A Witness of Love

by

Anne Kristalin Spanfelner

Publishers Note

    As the publisher of Endurance Press I strive to help authors bring their stories and books to life. Anne is a talented young author who weaves a moving story of redemption in this book. As with a lot of redemptive stories there are tough topics explored in these pages. These topics may be triggering to young children, or anyone who has struggled through abuse in their past.

    Please read *A Witness of Love* with discernment. My prayer is that you enjoy the story, learn from it, and grow.

Sincerely,

Robert
Publisher
Endurance Press

Acknowledgements

First and foremost, I thank God for this, and for giving me the strength to go on to the end.

I especially wish to thank my parents, Dan and Kristen, and my sisters, Nicole, Amber, and Autumn for the support, encouragement, and all the help they've given me over the years it has taken me to get here. Thanks also to all my family who encouraged me along the way.

I want to thank those who read my book and gave me feedback: Papa, Mom, Nicole, Rebekah, Liam, Claire, and Mrs. Christensen. Thank you all so much for all the time and hard work you put into reading and editing my manuscript!

Thanks to all who helped with the cover of my book. Cole, thanks for posing on the cover, cousin. Mrs. Howison, thank you for taking the pictures. Mr. Eric and Ms. Ellen, thank you for allowing us to use your pasture and your horses. And, thank you to the horses, Joe and Jubilee. Thank you all so much!

Thanks to all who supported me in their special ways, however it may have been. Thank you to Aunt Nancy for your advice. And thank you to Ms. Rene for your generous and kind support.

Thanks to Dr. Warner and his staff for all their help and support. Thank you, Dr. Warner!

To all who prayed for me during my most difficult times, thank you. To all my friends who encouraged me, thank you. I'd like to especially thank Elena, Rebekah, and James. Thanks also to my cousin, Paul, for his encouragement and advice.

I'd like to thank those who helped me with the publishing and editing itself. They have all been very kind and helpful as I worked to get my first book published. Thanks to my publisher, Robert Sweesy, and his wife, Christina. Mr. Sweesy was wonderful to work with through every step of the way! Mrs. Sweesy did an amazing job on the cover design! Thanks to the developmental editor, Cristen Iris, and to the copy-and-line editor, Carol Kjar. Thank you all! I appreciate all the help and encouragement you've given me during this journey!

Dedication

This book is dedicated to all you who feel unloved and hurt, who struggle and suffer. It is my deepest hope that this book will bring you comfort. Whoever you are, whatever you are going through, you, yes, even you, are loved. Don't give up. You are loved.

Chapter One

The morning sun glinted in a soft red glow against the beautiful masonry of the ranch house. A gentle breeze blew through the leaves of the ivy that bountifully climbed the east side of the ranch house. This was a promise of so beautiful and clear a spring day, one would be at peace just to feel the bright, dazzling red sun begin to gently warm the land.

As the rays of the morning sunshine began to flow through the window of dark-haired, pretty Anna Campbell, the young woman awoke for the third time that week from an awful nightmare. Horror and fear were the first feelings that struck her. She let out a weak sob and numbly brushed away the few tears that ran down her nose and wet her cheeks, hugging her long legs to her chest.

"Please, God, no!" she whispered, a catch in her throat. "Please, do not make me see such a thing!"

Slowly and tearfully, she arose and stood beside her window. Her lip trembled as she leaned her head against the sill. Tears still ran down her pale and horrified face. For a long time, she stood and gazed toward the sunrise. Visions of her sickening nightmare tore unbidden through her mind, and she could do nothing to take them away.

"Jack," she whispered. "Jack can take it away." A sudden desire to be in the arms of the ranch hand she cared for very much came over her, compelling her to turn away from the window to dress.

Minutes later, Anna walked through the still barnyard, listening for the familiar sound of the ranch hands doing early morning work. The large stretch of barnyard lay between the back of the ranch house and the barn. In the middle of it was a volleyball net, and closer to the ranch house was a basketball court. On the north side of the ranch house was an enclosed area for the swimming pool. The barnyard was always kept meticulously clean for boarding guests staying the summer.

Anna stopped to listen. All she could hear was the soft, gentle sound of the horses grazing in the pastures adjoining the barnyard. She gave a soft sigh in disappointment and turned to go back to her room on the first floor of the three-story ranch house.

Weary and still trembling from the nightmare, Anna lay on her bed. She pulled the quilt up to her shoulders and closed her eyes. A shaky sigh broke free and another tear rolled down her cheek. In the silent darkness of her mind, she heard a loud crack; from her nightmare. She uttered a short cry and cringed. Why couldn't she just erase such a terrible nightmare from her mind?

"Of course, sir," Liesel Campbell said into the phone. "When do you plan on arriving? Tomorrow? Yes, sir, that is a perfect time to arrive. You too. Goodbye."

Liesel hung up and wrote in a schedule which listed arrivals and departures of guests staying at the Campbell ranch. She too was dark haired, but not as tall as Anna. At that moment, she glanced up as her daughter entered the front room.

"Mom?" said Anna.

Liesel looked up from her work. "Oh, Anna," she murmured when she saw the look of distress on Anna's tear-stained face. "Not another one." She stretched out her arm for her daughter.

Anna came to stand by Liesel. Liesel put her arm around Anna's waist, and Anna put her head on Liesel's shoulder. "I can't stop them from coming, and I cannot make them go away. Mom, what am I going to do?" Her voice quivered as she spoke.

"Did you pray about it like I told you to?"

"Yes. But the same nightmare keeps coming."

Liesel decided to change the subject in the effort to take Anna's mind off the nightmare that haunted her. "I got a call from a family who wants to come to the ranch for the summer. The Smiths will be here tomorrow sometime in the afternoon. I'll need your help getting rooms ready."

"Of course, Mom," Anna replied as she let go of Liesel.

The sun had risen high in the sky when Anna returned to the barnyard after breakfast was over. A few guests took pleasure in horseback riding right after breakfast, and now the giant barnyard was no longer quiet as it had been at the break of dawn. It was alive with laughter and people calling to each other. Frustrated and tired of the noise, Anna struggled with her emotions. She felt a sudden urge to disappear and retreat to the safety and solitude of her special quiet place none of the guests knew about.

A golden colored mare lifted her head from grazing in the pasture at the approach of the troubled girl and stood quietly as Anna came to her. Anna let her hand gently stroke the mare's face. The mare remained still, allowing Anna to find a little comfort in her sun-warmed coat. After a minute of standing, Anna silently put a halter onto the mare and tied the ends of a lead rope to either side of the halter. "I desperately need to be alone for a while, Emerald," she said softly to her horse. "Almost all morning, I've been listening to the guests talking and laughing to each other, and I feel like crying."

Anna brushed at a tear and led Emerald out of the pasture. She mounted her horse bareback, and felt a slight sense of peace that perhaps, somehow, things would be all right.

Two miles away from the main part of the ranch was a secluded area where she often rode Emerald. The little spot Anna loved so much was a tiny valley containing a meadow beside a brook that never ceased its soft flowing. On the south side of the brook, a grove of weeping willow trees with long, tender branches drooped and lightly brushed the ground and the tops of grass. Thick, lush grass grew bountifully and richly under the willows and throughout the meadow. Anna loved this secluded, beautiful place and found time almost every day to think and pray and dream here.

She slid off Emerald's back and took the lead rope off the halter. Emerald trotted away, splashing across the brook to graze in the meadow. Anna gave a soft sigh and walked to one of the willow trees where her father had built a treehouse many years ago. She climbed the wooden ladder and sat on the edge of the ledge built onto the treehouse. Normally, she might have gone inside the tiny cabin-like treehouse, but today, she sat outside and stared down at the brook, letting her thoughts drift away in its quiet rush.

Anna sat for a long time, swinging her bare feet and trying to get rid of her fears. The peaceful scene was interrupted by the sound of another horse slowly and casually clip-clopping toward her.

Jack stopped his horse and looked up at her. "Your mother said I might find you here," he said. The sunlight shone on his brown hair.

A surge of relief and pleasure raced briefly through Anna. "Hi, Jack," she said. The sunlight on his hair made her think of an angel. *And angelic he is,* she thought to herself.

Jack dismounted and dropped his reins to the ground before climbing the ladder and sitting beside Anna. "Something wrong?" he asked, his tone holding concern.

Anna nodded. A sudden choke in her throat prevented her from speaking. She bowed her head.

"Anna, what's wrong?" he asked, looking her in the eyes

10

when she lifted her head.

"I've had an awful nightmare several times this week," she whispered, trying to keep her voice under control. She leaned against him and laid her head on his shoulder.

Jack put his arm around her. "Want to tell me about it?"

"I do, Jack," she replied, nodding. "It's about someone coming to stay at the ranch for the summer, but I don't know who they are. When I'm dreaming, I know exactly what they look like, but when I wake up, I can't remember. There is a boy, at least, I think it was a boy, I can't really remember for sure. It was awful, Jack. It's not a very clear dream. I could hear a strange, sharp crack over and over and over again. The poor boy was screaming and crying. It's pure agony just to hear him. The boy threw himself against me, and I could feel something warm and wet running all over my body. And then the boy fell down and died."

Jack squeezed her shoulders sympathetically, but was unsure of what to tell her. "I'm sorry, Anna," he murmured. "You know it isn't real, though, don't you?"

Anna couldn't keep the tears from falling. "I know it isn't, Jack, but I can't help feeling that it is. It all seems so real, even though I don't really know for sure what was happening." She turned her face pleadingly to the young ranch hand's eyes. "Jack, what am I going to do?"

Jack didn't know what to say. He squeezed her shoulder tighter.

Anna bowed her head, clutched her hands in her lap, and cried.

Jack waited quietly and said nothing as he rubbed her shoulder.

Eventually, Anna's tears slowed to a full stop, and she wearily lifted her hot face. Her head pounded.

"I'll take you home," Jack murmured after a while. He climbed down from the treehouse and offered a hand to Anna.

Anna accepted Jack's help down and tried to whistle for Emerald like she always did. But after crying, she found it impossible so she wearily crossed the creek to retrieve her horse.

They rode in silence across the miles home. Upon arriving at the main part of the ranch, the barnyard was still loud and alive, but Anna no longer felt frustrated by it. She let Emerald loose in the pasture, thinking of how grateful she was for Jack. If he hadn't come to be with her, she felt certain she would still be sunk in despair. Now, she felt ready to face the day, and able to put the nightmare behind her.

"Thank you for coming to talk to me, Jack," said Anna, giving the ranch hand a warm smile.

"You're welcome, Anna," Jack replied. "I hope you don't have that nightmare again."

Anna nodded wholeheartedly. "So do I."

Jack went into the ranch house to find Liesel. He tapped on the door jamb of the lobby, removing his hat as he stepped into the room.

Liesel looked up from her work. "Hi, Jack. Did you find her?"

"Yes, ma'am," Jack replied, fiddling with the brim of his hat. "You were right, she did want to talk to me. I'm not sure I was able to help her, though. I don't know why."

"I wouldn't worry about it, Jack. There are some things people can't help each other with, and some things they can."

Jack nodded, shoved his hat back on his head, and left the room.

Chapter Two

The ranch house stood proudly in the morning light of the next day. Inside, Anna and Liesel served breakfast to the guests before having their own breakfast. Liesel blew at a loose strand of her dark hair as she sat down beside Frank at the round table in the kitchen. Anna returned from serving in the dining room that adjoined the kitchen and sat at the table also.

"Tired, Liesel?" Frank asked. He looked at her out the corner of his blue eyes.

Liesel expelled her breath and nodded. "Yes, I am, Frank. There's a lot of cooking that goes into the meals for all these people."

Frank chuckled and ran his fingers through his dirt blond hair.

"When are the new guests coming today, Mom?" Anna asked as she served herself hot cereal from the middle of the table.

"Oh, I don't know," Liesel replied. She swiped at the strand of unruly dark hair. "The man said they'd get here sometime today. I hate it when guests don't have schedules. It drives me crazy."

"Liesel," Frank said as he finished a mouthful of his cereal. "I was thinking of giving a barnyard dance sometime soon. When do you think we could?"

"Anytime," Liesel replied absentmindedly.

"How about tonight?"

"Tonigh—Frank!" Liesel cocked her head and drew her eyebrows together in exasperation. "Tonight? Really?"

"Sure. Why not?"

"Isn't that too soon? That's kind of short notice."

Anna rested her chin in her hand, her eyebrows high in amusement as she watched her parents battle back and forth.

Frank pleaded on. He named a song Liesel liked very much. "I'll play it first."

Liesel twisted her lips, narrowed her green eyes, and lifted one eyebrow, the look that said, 'How do you talk me into these things?' It was the same look she always got whenever she reluctantly agreed to one of Frank's ideas.

"Good," Frank said, trying to suppress a laugh. "I'll get Jack and Jake to set up the lamp posts and clear the sport nets this afternoon. Anna, when you go through the rooms to tidy them up, will you put an invitation in each room?"

"Invitations?" Anna asked. She lifted an eyebrow.

"Yes. Print out some invitations and distribute them throughout the rooms."

"I'll do that right after breakfast," she replied. She couldn't help but feel rather excited for the dance. She knew who her partner would be for most of the evening, and the thought of dancing dance after glorious dance with Jack made her heart leap with anticipation.

Later, when Anna was putting an invitation to the dance in one of the third-story rooms for the new guests, she heard her mother's voice in the hall. "Right over here, Mr. Smith. I have three rooms set up. Will that be enough?"

Liesel turned into the room Anna was in. "Here's one of the rooms I have for you," she continued.

A graying man of a medium height and slightly stocky stature followed Liesel into the room. "Two rooms will be enough, Mrs. Campbell," he said cheerfully. "Here we are, Polly," he called out the door.

A very slender woman with lines of age on her cheeks and veins showing on her slim hands came in behind her husband. She had her silver hair neatly kept back in a bun and had on a pretty pair of earrings. She had wire-frame glasses perched gently on her nose.

"Each room has a bathroom, extra towels, sheets, and plenty of wardrobe space," said Liesel. "If you need anything more, feel free to let us know. Oh, Mr. Smith, this is my daughter, Anna. Anna, this is Mr. Smith and his wife, Polly."

"Hello," Anna greeted. Already she liked the easy, cheerful attitude about the Smiths. And yet, she felt a strange sense that she had seen them somewhere before.

Liesel turned back to Mr. Smith. "Are you sure two rooms are all that's necessary, Mr. Smith? You have three boys."

"We'll get along very well, thank you, ma'am," Mr. Smith replied. "Boys! We'll let you have this room, and your mom and I will take the room at the end of this hall. It's right next to yours."

Two muscular, red-haired men entered the room. "Anything you say, Dad," said one.

Anna cocked her head. The young men looked shockingly similar! How would she learn to tell the difference between them?

"Ms. Campbell, these are my sons, Esau on the left, and Saul on the right."

"Are they twins?" Liesel asked with a smile.

"Yes, ma'am," Mr. Smith replied with a grin.

"How old are they?"

"Twenty-three."

"Do you really think just two rooms will be enough, Timothy?" asked Polly.

"Of course, Polly," he answered. "They can get along on one bed, can't you boys?"

"Absolutely," said Saul.

A movement from behind the twins caught Anna's eye. Timothy turned his head as though to see something which remained behind the twins. "This is my other boy." He reached behind and took someone by the arm.

A shy young man hesitantly came out from behind Esau and Saul. Timothy gripped his shoulder as he kept his eyes on the floor as though he were lost in thought. "This is Colsson."

When Anna saw the youngest son, she struggled to hide a gasp. Colsson was the skinniest living creature she had ever seen! His clothing hung loosely from his shoulders, and she could plainly see his ribs through his tucked-in shirt. His jaw looked sharp and angled. He had light blond hair and blue-green eyes. He was tall, making him look even thinner.

Anna forced herself to smile. "Nice to meet you all," she said, trying to keep her face straight and her voice from shaking at the shock of seeing Colsson.

Anna tossed a look at her mother. Liesel shared her glance, telling her that her mother knew she felt a little awkward over Colsson's stature and appearance.

"Well, we'll let you all get settled before lunch. Lunch is at noon every day," said Liesel, clearing her throat in an inept sort of manner.

"How do we get to the dining room?" asked Polly.

"Go down the stairs we just came up," Liesel instructed. "When you reach the first floor, take a right turn down the hall and go past the lobby. The dining room is the room adjoining it."

"And what's the room to the left of the lobby?" asked Saul.

"That's the living room," Liesel replied.

"Got it," said Timothy.

"Do you have any questions? Anything else you need to know?"

"I think we're good, thank you," Timothy glanced all around at the others as he spoke.

"Ready, Anna?" asked Liesel.

Anna nodded and followed her mother out of the room. Once safely down the hall and almost to the stairs, Anna let out her breath and put her hand on her heart.

"It's nothing to worry about, Anna," said Liesel. "He's just naturally that way."

"He's so skinny," Anna whispered. "Poor guy."

"I had a little bit of a start when I first saw him, too. I think it's okay. Some teenage boys are just naturally skinny."

"That skinny?" Anna whispered in a hoarse shriek.

"I don't recall seeing a teenage boy that skinny before, but all people are different. Don't let it bother you, okay?"

"I'll try, Mom."

Anna and Liesel went into the kitchen to start the midday meal.

"I feel like I've seen them somewhere before," said Anna as she began cutting lettuce. She squinted, trying to place where she had seen them.

"You do?" asked Liesel.

"Yeah. I'm not sure where, though."

"Hmm. You must have met them somewhere else. They don't seem familiar to me at all."

Anna paused in her cutting to close her eyes. She shook her head. It wasn't any use. She couldn't remember where she had seen the Smith family.

A little while later, as Anna was placing the courses on the table, the Smith family came down and sat at the table. She watched Colsson out of the corner of her eye as she began serving food to the Smiths. He didn't make eye contact with anyone, but focused his gaze on the empty plate before him. Anna picked up his plate and started to serve him. "How much do you want?"

"Uh—" Colsson stammered. "I don't know, I—" He threw a very brief glance at his father who was introducing himself to someone sitting next to him. Brief as the glance was, Anna still saw it. "More, please," he whispered so faintly Anna could hardly hear him.

An uninvited tingle crept up Anna's spine. She heaped more onto his plate and set it down. Almost before she had taken her fingers off the plate, Colsson shoveled the biggest bite he could into his mouth.

Bewildered at the strange boy's actions, Anna left to return to the kitchen. "Man alive, he must be hungry. You should have seen the size of the first bite he took."

"Who?" asked Liesel.

"The new guy, Colsson. I think he's as hungry as he is shy."

"Growing boys usually are, Anna. He's probably about your age."

"Nineteen? He seems younger than that."

Liesel shrugged. "Maybe he is, and maybe he isn't."

"Just seems weird," Anna murmured to herself. "It doesn't add up."

Liesel paused her work. "Anna, I wouldn't let my imagination run away with me."

"I'm not letting my imagination run away with me, Mom," Anna replied. "I've just never seen anyone that skinny, and it makes me nervous."

"Nervous about what?"

"I don't know, it just does."

"Well, try not to worry about it." Liesel smiled at Anna. "I don't see anything wrong. Is that helpful?"

Anna nodded and smiled back. "I think so, Mom." Inwardly, she resolved to do what her mother told her. She managed to rid herself of what she now considered her ridiculous thoughts. She chuckled to herself and wondered how she could have thought such things.

After dinner that evening, Anna went up to the third floor to tell the Smiths about the dance in case they hadn't seen the invitation or didn't know how to find the barnyard. She first told Timothy and Polly, who told her they would certainly join, and then she knocked at the boys' door. She heard a faint 'Come in' and opened the door. Colsson was sitting alone in the room.

"Hi," she said as she stood in the doorway. "I just wanted to let you know there is a dance this evening at eight o'clock in the barnyard. Would you like to join?"

Colsson dropped his gaze to the floor. "I don't know. I don't know how to dance."

"It's easy," she replied, chuckling slightly. "I can show you if you want."

"I don't know if I can go. Depends on whether or not my parents decide to take me."

"You could come by yourself if you wanted to," said Anna. She walked past Colsson and opened the window overlooking the barnyard.

Colsson stood and walked to the window to look. He leaned over the top of Anna to see what she was indicating.

"It's just right down there."

Colsson leaned a little farther, holding onto the side of the window for support. Crouched next to the window, Anna felt her shoulder lightly touching his body. A tingle shot down her spine when she felt how thin he was. She forced herself to turn her attention back to the barnyard.

People were laughing and shouting raucously. Some crowded around the basketball hoop, some played volleyball, some played badminton, and some simply stood around talking or introducing themselves to other people.

Colsson pointed down to the barnyard busy with activity. "Down there?"

"Yes," Anna turned her head and smiled broadly up at him. "You should go. It's the most wonderful thing."

Colsson backed away from the window. Anna's smile slipped. There was something troubling him. It was written in his blue-green eyes. He stared at the wall, as though his mind were far away. His eyes twitched, and his upper lip moved slightly.

"Colsson?"

Colsson gave a startled gasp and his body jerked. "I can't go!" he whispered.

"You are entitled to privacy, but may I ask why? Is something wrong?"

His eyes closed again, and his face twitched, as though he were seeing something horrifying, or battling fiercely with himself. "Nothing's wrong," he murmured in a low tone.

Anna took a step toward him. "Can I help?"

Right as she moved and spoke, Colsson jerked again and uttered an alarmed cry. He held his arm high, and turned his head away, gritting his teeth. Anna stood still, numb with shock. Her thoughts swirled. Colsson, standing right there in front of her, holding his arm up as though he thought she would hit him!

Colsson seemed to realize what he was doing. He dropped his arm and turned back. Anna could see his face again, and that look in his eyes was *still* there, only it had worsened.

"S-sorry," Colsson murmured. "Believe me, I did not mean to do that."

"It's okay," she whispered assuredly. "I promise."

"I startle easy. I have for as long as I can remember. Please don't take it seriously."

"I won't," Anna found herself saying. Distrust, though she did not know from whence it came nor why it did, came over her. She forced herself to change the subject. "About the dance? Why couldn't you go?"

"I haven't anything to wear."

"You don't have to wear anything special. Nobody is going to be wearing anything fancy. Most of the men will have their regular clothes on, and most of the girls will be wearing skirts or dresses. We do all kinds of dances, like English Country dances, line dances, twists, tangos, swings, and music like that. All you do is go outside and ask somebody to dance. That's all there is to it. Mostly the dances will be waltzes, but there will be some when you can move any way you want to. You can dance, or you can just watch."

"I don't know how to do any of that," said he sadly.

"The English Country dances will have practices before they put on the music."

"Well, how do you do it?"

"I'll show you how to waltz if you want," she offered.

He hesitated. "Okay," he gave in with a whisper. But the troubled look in his eyes remained.

"Come over here," she instructed, moving to the middle of the floor.

Colsson stood where she showed him.

"Put your right hand on my low back," she began. She guided his hand to the right place. "Hold your arm out." As he held his other arm out, Anna put her hand in his. "Bend your arm a little bit," she said, gently tugging on his hand to get his arm to bend.

"This way?" he asked awkwardly.

"That's right," Anna encouraged. "Now, take a small step forward with your left foot."

Watching his feet, he took an awkward, somewhat shaky step.

"Now step to the side using your right foot, and step together."

Colsson clutched her hand tightly, and she saw beads of sweat forming on his forehead. His face now looked anxious. He stepped together stiffly and firmly.

"Relax," she murmured. "The whole idea of this dance is to be loose and light."

Colsson exhaled, keeping his eyes on his feet. His grip on her hand didn't loosen.

"Step back with your right foot, to the side with your left, step together. Forward with your left, side, together. Back, side, together. Forward, side, together."

"You do this the whole time?" he asked a minute later.

"No, not the whole time. This is only the 'box waltz'. Once you get used to doing this, you can start doing turns in every direction all around the dance floor."

"Turns?" He repeated, his voice very unsure, and to Anna, it sounded strained.

"You use the same basic steps you're doing here, only you're moving and turning in all different directions. I'll give you little pushes and pulls to guide you through; you just have to keep doing this same pattern."

A few minutes later, Anna guided Colsson to move about the room using the same pattern she had just shown him. They didn't get very far before he got mixed up.

"Let's start over," Anna suggested patiently. She led him back to the middle of the room, and they began again with the box waltz.

Colsson was just getting the hang of waltzing when the door opened and one of the twins came in. Anna's back was turned when he entered, but when she saw Colsson's mouth drop open and he let go of her hand, she turned around. He tripped and fell backward onto the floor. "Saul!" he exclaimed.

"What on earth is going on?" asked Saul. He stared at the two of them, his eyes wide in astonishment.

"I—I—" Colsson stammered. He couldn't tear his eyes from his brother. "Wh—when did you come in?"

"Just now," Saul replied as if Colsson were dumb.

"I'm just showing him how to waltz," Anna spoke up. "There's a dance tonight in the barnyard."

Colsson slowly stood. "She's showing me how to dance in case I go tonight."

"I'd better get going," said Anna. She went toward the door.

Saul followed her into the hall. "Just so you know, I seriously doubt Colsson will be going tonight," he whispered.

"Why is that?" Anna whispered back.

"He's very shy and doesn't like to be around other people."

"He acted like he wanted to go. He didn't know how to dance. That's why I was showing him how."

"I know, but I know Colsson. He's not going to want to go. I hope you understand."

"Of course," said Anna, wishing she could confidently say so. "See you later." She left, and she heard the door close.

As the sun was setting, couples and families began gathering for the first dance.

"Hey, Anna," Jack called. He jogged over to her. "Can I have this dance?"

"Of course," Anna replied heartily. She took his hand as he led her out to the dance floor.

Enraptured in dancing with Jack, Anna did not notice a dejected, lonely creature resting his arms on the sill of his window and looking out over the lively dancing.

Song after song was played, and Jack asked Anna to dance to almost every one. During the faster dances, Jack's brown hair constantly mussed and fell over his forehead. Anna loved to see it and laughed out loud as she tried to fix his hair whenever she had a slight chance to do so. She swore Jack deliberately tried to mess up his hair. He had the widest grin on his face as he tossed his head and bounced through the other couples as soon as she fixed it. They would meet again, Anna would laugh, and smooth his hair back. As she twirled with Jack, Anna felt that she cared for Jack above anything else in the world.

During one of the waltzes, Jack had his arms around Anna's waist. Anna rested her hands on Jack's shoulders. They moved slowly around the dance floor, dancing with foreheads gently touching and eyes closed.

"Anna," Jack whispered.

"Yes," she replied, her voice also in a whisper.

"I talked to your father this afternoon. I have his permission to enter courtship with you, if only you are willing."

"Yes!" she cried. Her heart swelled with happiness uncontained. "Yes, I'm willing!"

Jack held her even closer. "I'm glad," he said softly. He paused in the dance and held the side of her face, his blue eyes looking straight into her green ones. "You don't know how glad."

Anna smiled and laid her head against his shoulder.

After the dance was over and everything was put away from the barnyard, Jack whistled one of the dance tunes as he and

Jake walked to the bunkhouse next to the north pastures. He flopped lengthwise on his bed and let out an energetic sigh.

"Man, Jake, I sure had some amazing dances tonight. I'm telling you, I think I've fallen head over heels in love with that girl."

Jake smiled at Jack. "You know she's only nineteen, Jack. You're twenty-two. I don't know if the boss is going to let you start courting her yet."

Jack sat up and swung his legs off the side of the bed. "I've got news for you, big brother." His face broke out in a broad grin. "I asked Frank this afternoon about courting her. And he said yes!"

Jake sat on the edge of his bed right next to Jack's and began peeling off his boots. "I'm happy for you, Jack. I can tell that you are in fact in love with her. But—" his voice trailed off and an odd expression came over his face.

"But?" Jack wrinkled his forehead, a nervous tingle creeping through his fingertips.

"I don't know." Jake set his boot on the floor and looked at Jack, a faraway look in his eyes. "I just can't quite see her as my sister-in-law somehow."

"You'll get used to it in time, Jake. Don't worry."

"I suppose I will," Jake grunted softly and went back to undressing.

Chapter Three

"Good morning," Anna greeted the boarders as she entered the dining room from the kitchen. All the boarders echoed in unison. They were laughing and talking amongst themselves about the dance the previous night. They joked of mess ups they had made in some of the dances. Anna carried a platter full of pancakes to the table on the left side of the dining room. As she set it down, she looked all around the table, feeling as though someone were missing. It didn't take her long to realize who.

"Where's Colsson?" she asked Timothy.

"He wasn't feeling very well this morning, so he stayed upstairs." Timothy didn't stop eating.

Anna's heart skipped a beat. "Is he okay?"

"He'll be fine," Esau said nonchalantly as he leaned back in his chair giving a confident chuckle. Or was it Saul? Anna couldn't tell.

Anna leaned in close to Timothy to avoid being heard. "Is he getting sick? Is there anything I can do?"

"We don't know for sure," Timothy replied, whispering back. "I just think he's too shy."

"He probably needs to sleep for a while," said Polly. "That might be all it is."

"Please don't worry your pretty little head about him," said Timothy, giving her a self-assured smile.

Anna said no more and returned to the warmth of the kitchen. "Colsson isn't out there, Mom."

Liesel looked up from the griddle and swatted steam away from her face. "Where is he?"

"He's upstairs. The Smiths mentioned he said he wasn't feeling well, but they also said they thought it could be because he's shy."

"Do they want us to do anything for him?"

"They said not to worry about him."

Liesel was quiet. Anna searched her mother's face. Liesel hallowed her cheeks and drew her eyebrows together. "After breakfast, why don't you go up and ask him how he is."

For some odd reason, Anna felt her shoulders slump in relief. "Right away."

When she went back to the dining room with pancakes for the other table, she heard the Smiths talking to some of the others at their table, discussing their plans for the day. When one of the twins suggested going on a fishing trip to a small lake about ten miles from the main part of the ranch, the rest of the family agreed heartily to the plan. Polly wanted to travel to the destination on horseback instead of taking the car over the dirt road.

Upon hearing of the plan, Anna offered, "I'll ask my mom to pack a lunch for you if you like."

"That would be most appreciated," Polly replied as she cautiously picked up her steaming coffee cup. "Thank you."

Immediately after the Smiths left on their all-day trek, Anna went upstairs at her mother's request to check on Colsson. As she listened for a minute at the door, she was startled to hear a soft sound from inside, as though someone were weeping.

Anna rapped gently on the door. "Are you okay, Colsson?"

"Who—who is it?" asked a weak voice from inside.

"It's me, Anna. Your family said you weren't feeling well this morning, so I came to check on you. May I come in?"

"The door's locked," said Colsson, barely audible.

She flipped through a set of keys she carried and inserted the right key into the lock, turning the knob as she did so.

Colsson was lying on his side on the floor when Anna entered. "Why are you on the floor?" she asked, suddenly alarmed. "Are you hurt? Did you fall?"

He shook his head as he pushed himself onto his elbow and brushed his other arm across his eyes. His face was flushed, and his eyes were very red. He had been weeping for a while. He snuffled through his clogged nose, making a deep, short sound as he pushed himself to a sitting position.

Anna crossed the room to stand beside him. What was going on? She started to sit on the bed.

"Don't sit on the bed!" he suddenly cried.

Startled, she straightened abruptly. "What's wrong?"

He didn't answer right away but stared at the neatly made bed.

She knelt to look the young man in the eyes. "Colsson, why aren't you sleeping on the bed instead of the floor?"

Colsson dropped his gaze to the floor. He reached up with both hands and clutched his hair. "Esau and Saul don't want the bed messed up. They can tell if I've been on it."

"Is that all?" she asked with a tone implying that this statement was utterly ridiculous. "It's just as much your bed as theirs." She threw her hands in the air in exasperation.

Colsson let out a short cry, threw his arms over his head, and cowered into a tight ball on the floor.

Struck with surprise at his motion, she questioned cautiously, "Colsson?"

"Don't hurt me!" he cried, his voice muffled.

"Colsson, I won't hurt you," Anna whispered gently. She knelt next to him, cautiously reached out her hand, and tenderly brushed a strand of his blond hair back, which had fallen over his forehead.

Slowly, Colsson uncoiled and took his arms away from his head and shoulders. He kept his eyes on Anna the whole time.

"What made you think I would hurt you?"

He shrugged, unable and unwilling to say anything more.

Colsson stood and stiffly walked to the bathroom to wash his face. Anna let out a sigh and looked down. Something white peeked out from under the edge of the bed. A puzzled expression crossed her face. She leaned over from her sitting position to pick it up. It was a set of sheets! Why were these under the bed? She knew they hadn't been there the previous day.

As Anna straightened out the crumpled sheets, a red spot caught her eye. She spread the sheet over her lap the best she could. Besides the one spot, more like it varying in size revealed themselves. Some spots were small and numerous, and in some places, patches were bigger than her hand. It was blood!

She looked in the direction of the bathroom door.

The door was open, and Colsson stood in front of the sink, fidgeting with the towel.

"Colsson, are you okay?" she called to him.

He slowly came out of the bathroom. "I suppose so."

Anna wrinkled her eyebrows, looking steadily at Colsson. "You suppose?" she repeated. "Do you mean to tell me you don't know?"

"Why?" He walked toward her.

Her eyes again became fixated on the sheets. "I just found these under the bed. Did something happen in the night?"

His eyes widened at the sight of the sheets. "Not in so far as

I am aware," he said hastily. He turned and went away quickly.

"What about Esau and Saul?" she asked. "Are they okay?"

"They're fine," he said in a brusque manner.

Anna stood, undecided on what she should do and still unnerved about the sheets. However, she knew she needed to talk to her mother about it as soon as she could. She forced herself to speak. "Are you feeling well enough to eat?"

"Yes—no," he sighed and turned back around to face her. "My family thinks I shouldn't eat. At least, for a while."

"I'm not so sure. Not that I'm doubting your family's judgment, but in my experience, I've found it's sometimes better to eat for the sake of fighting off whatever sickness it is. You, in my opinion, need to eat." She held up the sheets. "Especially if you bled in the night."

"Wait a minute, what makes you think it was me?" he asked, crossing his arms.

"First of all, you are very convinced that Esau and Saul are fine. Secondly, you just stammered. You didn't give me a positive answer concerning my question of 'Are you okay'. There was doubt in your own words."

He shut his mouth and glared at her.

"What is going on, Colsson?" Anna asked a bit more gently. "What happened?"

He dropped his eyes and twisted the hem of his thin shirt. "Nothing," he whispered.

"I don't believe you, Colsson," said Anna in a gentle but warning tone.

He kept his head cocked as he stared at the shirt he fiddled with. No reply passed his lips.

The feeling that something was wrong grew stronger within Anna. The feeling was so severe, she ached all over.

She forced herself to change the subject after a moment of awkward silence. "There are leftovers from breakfast I can heat up for you." She turned to leave.

"I can't," Colsson called desperately.

Anna turned back around. "And why not?"

"I was told not to leave here," he replied, turning away. "If I were seen by my family, they'll want to know why I am up and not...resting." His voice trailed off at the last word.

"Oh yeah. Because you're sick, right?" Anna slapped a fist on her hip and drew her eyebrows together.

"If you're worried about me being sick, don't be," he said harshly. He scowled.

"Then why are you up here still? Because your family thinks you *are* sick? Or are you too cowardly to decide for yourself?"

He slung his head around, his hair flinging with the toss. His eyes flashed fiercely.

"Colsson, how old are you?"

"Nineteen."

"You're old enough to make your own decisions, for Pete's sake. You're an adult."

"I'm just a boy. A boy who doesn't know any better and needs to be told what to do."

Anna frowned. "Says who?"

"My dad, mostly."

"Colsson, *I'm* nineteen. Neither my mom nor my dad is going to object or be upset if I decide to get up and eat something. I'm not under that kind of restriction."

His eyes darkened. "*I* am."

The fierce frown on his face and the bitterness in his voice startled Anna.

"Well, you don't need to be," she said in a softer tone.

32

"Besides, your parents are gone for the day. They won't know the difference, even if it mattered. Normally, I don't believe in deceiving anyone, but you are for a fact old enough to decide for yourself. Here's another thing. You don't really look like anything is wrong with you."

Taken aback, he bit his lip and cracked his knuckles. Sweat stood out on his forehead. Every move he made implied to Anna that he was nervous and maybe even scared.

Of what? Anna asked herself as she went to the door. To Colsson she said, "You're free to come down anytime, Colsson. It's your own choice, but you are more than welcome to come down." She slowly pulled the door closed behind her and went downstairs to the laundry room across from the kitchen.

Anna dropped the sheets in front of the washer and went into the kitchen where her mother was loading the dishwasher. "Mom, would you mind coming to see this?"

"What is it?" asked Liesel, straightening from loading the dishwasher.

Liesel followed her into the laundry room. Anna turned on the light. She picked up the sheets and spread them out to show Liesel the blood splotches. "Colsson must have bled in the night."

"Anna, what on earth makes you think it was Colsson?" asked Liesel.

"I was upstairs checking on him like you told me to. He was lying on the floor when I went in, crying. After talking to him for a few minutes, I found these sheets under the bed. I asked if he was okay, and he said, 'I suppose so'. I told him I found sheets under the bed and asked if anything had happened in the night, he said not that he was aware of. Then I asked if Esau and Saul were okay. 'They're fine,' he said."

Liesel frowned when she heard Anna imitate Colsson's tone. "This doesn't make any kind of sense. Why would he talk like that?"

Anna felt a strong sense of relief that this time, her mother was on her side. "That isn't all. When I came in, I started to sit on the bed, and he sort of gasped and yelled at me not to. When I asked why, he said Esau and Saul didn't want him on the bed. He said they could tell whether or not he had been on it. And a little later, I asked if he wanted to come down to get something to eat. I got the reply, 'I was told not to leave here. If my family sees me, they'll want to know why I'm not resting'. And, he's nineteen years old."

Liesel's mouth dropped open. "What?" she exclaimed. "That can't be. Doesn't he know he's legally an adult?"

"I told him, but he said he was just a boy who needs to be told what to do. I told him you and Dad wouldn't make me stay in my room, and that I wasn't under that kind of restriction. '*I am*', he said."

Liesel frowned again. "Why?"

"I have no idea, and he wouldn't say, but I wanted to tell you so you know what I found out."

"It doesn't make any kind of sense. The Smiths seem to be really nice people, but this can't be ignored. The only question is, what to do about it. Maybe I'll ask the Smiths later about the sheet deal and a bit more about Colsson."

"I invited him to come down. I also told him that he didn't look sick."

"If he comes down, let me know. I want to talk to him for myself."

About fifteen minutes later, when Anna was wiping down the two tables in the dining room, Colsson came timidly creeping in. She watched him out the corner of her eye. Sweat stood out on his forehead as he closed the door behind him. He walked with short jerks in his steps, and the same scared look that had been in his eyes the previous evening was back.

"I'm glad you decided to come down finally," she commented. "I left a place for you at the table."

Colsson sank into the indicated seat at the table and let out a small sigh.

Anna hurried into the kitchen. "He's down!" she said as she retrieved the plate of leftover pancakes. Liesel followed her back to the dining room.

"How much would you like?" Anna asked Colsson.

"All of what's there, please," he murmured.

Anna held her tongue from remarking how much it was. She gave him all he asked for.

"Thank you," he said, giving her a shy smile.

Liesel stood to the side of Colsson as he shoveled in the first bite. "While you are eating, Colsson, I need to talk to you. Anna just brought down some rather bloody sheets and told me about the conversation between you and her. I want you to know while I respect your privacy, I also kind of need to know what happened with the sheets."

Without lifting his head, Colsson replied, "I don't want to talk about it."

Anna bit her lip. Liesel raised an eyebrow. "Would your parents or brothers be willing to tell me?"

Colsson shook his head.

"I want to help you in whatever way is necessary. But I can't do that without help from you."

"I don't need help."

Anna and Liesel exchanged glances. Liesel left the dining room.

Anna returned to her job of wiping the tables down while Colsson practically inhaled his food. Something strange was going on, but what? Nothing was adding up. *Was* something going on?

"Have you been shown outside yet, Colsson?" Anna asked a couple minutes later.

Colsson shook his head, still not looking up. "No."

"I can show you if you like."

"But where's my family? Are you sure they're not here?" This time, he lifted his face to see her.

"They're out on an all-day trail ride. Why are you wondering?"

"Oh, nothing." he said the last word in a rush as he looked back down at his plate.

Anna pulled out a chair from the table behind Colsson and straddled it, folding her arms over the back of the chair and resting her chin on them. She stared at his back. "Colsson, what's bothering you?"

Colsson turned around and their eyes met. The frightened look had disappeared, replaced by a soft, almost crushed look. "Nothing's wrong. Nothing that can be understood."

Anna bit her tongue from persisting. She dropped her eyes to evade his gaze.

"I'm sorry," he whispered.

Anna lifted her eyes again. The expression in his eyes made her want to cry. She swallowed, trying to get rid of the lump in her throat.

"I can't—I can't explain this. I can't." He turned back.

Anna drew in her breath, striving to find strength to speak. A minute passed before she could. "Would you like to go outside when you're finished? You might like to participate in some of the activities."

"Activities?" he asked, sounding unsure. "What kind of activities?"

"Some people like to play volleyball, badminton, or basketball. We have a swimming pool too, and that's a favorite thing to do."

"I don't know how to do any of that."

"Well, there's a first time for everything. Are you willing to try?"

Colsson nodded and gave her a tiny smile, indicating that he must have been encouraged by her words.

Feeling her old self returning, Anna smiled back. "We'll go when you're done." She left him to finish eating.

Anna reported to Liesel everything said between them.

Liesel hallowed her cheeks. "I am going to talk to your father about it, and we'll see what he thinks. In the meantime, let me know everything you find out."

Anna led Colsson out the back door into the barnyard. All across the broad expanse of the barnyard, boarders were playing sports, swimming in the closed off area for the pool, laughing and calling to each other, and having a wonderful time.

"What would you like to see first?" she asked.

"I don't know," Colsson replied.

Anna started walking toward the volleyball net. "Hi, Terra!" she called. "How's the game coming on?"

A lady with russet red hair turned around and wiped sweat off her forehead. "Well, we're winnin', but this heat is startin' to take a toll on us. I think we're goin' to head over to the pool for a cool-down before the next match."

"She's the best volleyball player here," Anna explained to Colsson. "If you're going to play volleyball, you want to be on her side or else you're going to lose. Believe me. I tried on the other team and didn't do so good."

Colsson managed a tiny smile, but inside he felt lost and frightened.

Anna led him away from the busy barnyard and went into the pasture. As they walked, both people and horses stopped to stare at the skinny boy walking alongside Anna. Anna gave no indication of noticing, but Colsson felt every pair of eyes turn to watch him. He exhaled softly when Anna closed the gate behind them. They were a fair distance from the laughter and shouting now. All the people were a blur, and the noise had died down considerably.

"It's a bit quieter over here," said Anna. "Not completely, but if you want even more quiet, I can take you to a place where it is."

Colsson gave her another tiny smile but remained silent. Anna stopped next to Emerald. Although still living in a silent world of his own, he quietly drew near to Emerald and gently stroked her face. As if she could somehow understand his hidden troubles, Emerald stood still, her head turned slightly toward him standing at her neck, not even swishing her tail. He reached under Emerald's neck to pet under her white mane on the other side while continuing to stroke her face. As he let his hand slide down Emerald's nose, he found comfort in her coat, and in the largeness of the horse's body, he felt safe, like she could hide him from any danger, fear, or trouble. He never wanted to leave. He wished he could somehow stay there forever.

Anna stood and watched him pet the mare for a long time. She wanted so much to say something, but something prevented her, and therefore left the silence undisturbed as she watched his interactions with her mare. His tense shoulders relaxed, and for the first time since arriving on the ranch, he seemed at ease.

"You're very good with horses," Anna finally said, ten minutes later. "Do you ride a lot?"

"I've never touched a horse before." He held his fingers near Emerald's nose, who calmly breathed on his hand.

"Would you like to learn how to ride?"

"I don't know. I do, but I don't know if I should."

"How do you mean?" Anna felt apprehension growing again.

"Yes, I would like to learn," he said, evading her question.

"Alright. I'll get her halter and take her to the corral on the north side of the barn. I can saddle her there and show you how to ride."

Anna left him with Emerald and went to get the halter and lead rope. He was still stroking her when she returned. She put the halter on Emerald and led the mare out of the pasture to the corral. Anna saddled and bridled her, then led her into the middle of the corral.

"First thing, always be alert on the back of a horse," Anna began. "Anything can happen in just a second. It's too danger-ous to let your mind slip away. Same thing as driving a car."

Colsson nodded but a confused expression crossed his face.

"What is it?"

"I don't know how to drive."

She raised an eyebrow and continued. "To mount, stand on the left side of the horse. Put your left foot into the stirrup..." She lifted her foot up to it. "...which is where your feet stay whenever you're in the saddle. Have one hand on the cantle..." she gripped the back of the saddle, "...and the other hand hold-ing the horn." She pointed at the front of the saddle. "Hoist yourself up, swing your leg over the back of the saddle and sit down." With an easy motion, she mounted Emerald. "Then you slide your other foot into the other stirrup. It's as easy as that."

She jumped down. "Go ahead, Colsson. Give it a try."

Cautiously and hesitantly, he walked in jerky steps toward Emerald. Anna held onto the reins and watched him carefully. He reached up a shaky hand and took hold of the horn, then grabbed the cantle. He blew air from his cheeks as he struggled to get his foot in the stirrup. The muscles in his arms showed through his flesh as he worked to pull himself upward. He grunted with effort. Several efforts failed, but he finally man-aged to seat himself in the saddle. The hint of a smile crept into his countenance.

"Good work, Colsson!" Anna smiled before she went on. "Always important, keep the stirrups only at the ball of your feet. That way it's easier to slide out should there be a problem."

He looked from one side to the next, wiggling his feet to the right position.

"When you want her to go, give her a gentle kick in the sides with your heels. When you want her to turn, pull your hand holding the reins the direction you want to turn so you're touching the other side of her neck with the rein. But be very careful to be gentle. There is a bit in the horse's mouth that controls her. If you pull too hard, it'll be very painful to her. Okay?"

"Always gentle," he repeated softly. He tenderly stroked Emerald's neck as if assuring the mare that he understood and would always be careful to abide by this rule.

"When you want her to stop, pull the reins back toward you, remembering what I just told you about the bit." She motioned with her hand, moving it toward her chest. Satisfied she had covered everything she needed to tell him about riding, she put the reins over Emerald's head and laid them in his palm. A look of hesitance crossed his face. "It's okay," she murmured. "I promise." Gently, she closed his fingers over the reins.

"I won't forget about the bit," he murmured, never taking his eyes off the reins in his hands. "I know what it must be like."

The heat from the summer morning escaped Anna and a cold, utterly wretched feeling replaced it. A shiver shook her whole body. "What do you mean?" she asked, barely able to force the words out. "Why do you say you know?"

Colsson avoided her eyes. "What next?"

Her jaw feeling numb, Anna managed to say, "I'll lead you around for a few minutes until you get the hang of the saddle. Give her a little kick with your heels."

Colsson gave such a little tap with his heels, he hardly moved, and Emerald didn't even flinch.

"You can kick her a little harder," said Anna, her own voice sounding strange.

He gave the mare a slightly harder nudge. As he did, a strange look crossed his face, as though he didn't want to kick her at all. Anna gave a slight tug on Emerald's bridle to encourage the mare to move. Still wondering, and fearing, over Colsson's words, she led the mare around the corral so he could get the feel for being on Emerald's back.

"What's her name?" Colsson asked a few minutes later.

"Emerald."

"Emerald," Colsson repeated quietly. He stroked Emerald's neck.

"Are you enjoying your stay at the ranch so far?" As soon as the words left her mouth, she knew it was a stupid thing to ask. It was obvious he wasn't.

He didn't answer right away. "I can't really say I am," he whispered as though he didn't want to say it at all.

Anna didn't press him any further, wishing she hadn't asked that question.

When the lesson ended, Anna returned her horse to the pasture and walked with Colsson back to his room in the ranch house. She tried to get him to talk, conversing with him as much as she could, but no matter how hard she tried, no matter what questions she asked, she couldn't learn what troubled him.

They stopped outside the door to his room. "Thank you for showing me how to ride, Anna," he said. "I don't really get to do things like that."

"Well, maybe you can now that you're here," Anna said with heartfelt hope.

He shrugged his shoulders and looked at the floor. "I don't have hope for much change."

"I'll pray that you can," offered Anna.

Colsson lifted his eyes. "Pray?" he repeated. "What do you mean?"

"Pray to the Lord that you might be able to enjoy the time you have here."

He wasn't listening. He'd heard the one word that caused him to freeze entirely. His eyes grew wide and all the gentleness they had held while with Emerald disappeared, replaced with a cold look Anna never knew possible to have. He took a step back. "Don't say that Name to me!" he uttered in a low, threatening tone. "Ever!" He turned and ran into his room, slamming the door behind him.

Anna stood in the hall, numb with shock over Colsson's reaction. She couldn't believe what she just heard. Could this be what was troubling Colsson? Did he hold an anger against the Lord? Did his family keep him separate from Him?

Her thoughts twisting and turning like a steep mountain grade, she turned heel and raced for the stairs. Fear suddenly grew inside her and she no longer felt safe. She suddenly wanted to get as far away from the Smiths' rooms as possible.

When Anna entered the kitchen, out of breath, Liesel looked up from what she was doing. Her face took on a concerned expression. "Anna, what's wrong?"

Anna leaned against the door. "Colsson. I might have found out the reason for his strange behavior."

Liesel cocked her head. "Behavior?"

"He's been avoiding answering some of the questions I ask and saying things that don't make sense. The worst of it was a couple minutes ago." Anna told Liesel about her conversations with him and his reaction to her offer of prayer.

"I don't like it," Anna finished. "Some of the things he says just gives me the creeps. And he seems to be scared of his family."

"Scared of his family?"

"Yes. He keeps asking where his family is and worries about doing something other than his family wants him to do. Like leaving his room for instance."

"I don't like the sound of that." Liesel wrinkled her forehead. "But the Smiths seem like such a nice family. Why would he be afraid of them?"

"I don't know. That's what bothers me."

"Perhaps Frank and I ought to speak to them and ask for an explanation. Yet, they *are* entitled to privacy as long as there's obviously nothing seriously wrong, which seems to be the case right now. We don't know if there's anything wrong. Things just seem a little odd is all. There are odd things all around you, no matter where you look, no matter where you go. I guess what I'm saying is try not to worry about it too much. Colsson's an adult and can handle it."

"What about when he told me never to say the Lord's name? That isn't something to be ignored."

"You can't change him. You can't force him to be a Christian. The wisest thing you can do for now is to pray for him and be a good example for him."

Anna nodded. "I suppose you're right." Still, she couldn't shake the questions on her mind. Why did he hold such a deep anger against the Lord? And why was he afraid of his family?

Chapter Four

"Good morning, Colsson," Anna greeted him at the breakfast table. He didn't seem to hear her. He was fiddling with his fork like he was discouraged and unhappy.

She touched his shoulder. "Are you okay?"

Startled, he dropped his fork and jerked away. The fork dropped with a loud clatter, silencing everyone in the room. Colsson's jaw dropped, but no sound came out.

"Are you okay?" Anna repeated.

"He's just fine, Anna," said Polly, giving a smile. "He just wasn't expecting that."

Slowly the noise of the room returned to the usual chatter. Anna served everyone at the Smith's table. When she got around to Colsson's plate, she asked him, "How much do you want?"

Colsson kept his eyes on his plate. "I'm not hungry," he said through clenched teeth.

Anna couldn't believe what she just heard. "Are you sure?"

He nodded. The muscles in his jaw worked fiercely, and he squeezed his eyes shut tight.

Bewildered, Anna moved on to the next person. When she had finished the table, she returned to say something to Colsson. "Would you like to ride Emerald again after breakfast?"

"No," Colsson whispered hastily and flatly. "I'm going out with my family today." He turned his attention back to his empty plate.

After breakfast, Anna mounted Emerald and rode a few miles away to where she knew Jack would be working with some of the younger horses in the breaking pasture. Emerald cantered to the pasture, and at Anna's signal, stopped near the fence. Anna watched Jack for a few minutes. Jack skillfully lunged a young quarter horse in a circle around him and called commands. In his left hand, he held a long lead rein connected to the horse's halter.

After a few minutes, Jack called the young horse to stop. Anna dismounted and led Emerald into the pasture to where Jack petted and talked to the sweating horse. He looked up when Anna came to stand beside him. "Hi, Anna."

"Hi, Jack. Are you done for a few minutes?"

"Anything for you, sweetheart," he said with a smile. He held the lunging rein in his hand and wrapped his other arm around Anna's shoulders. "What's up?" he asked as they walked casually around the pasture.

Anna smiled and looked admiringly into Jack's face. "How did you know?"

"I know you better than you think, Anna," Jack replied with a grin. "I know something is up whenever you watch me like that."

"But you weren't even watching me! You had your back to me most of the time and you were focusing on the horse!"

Jack shrugged. "I just know. What is it?"

"Well, it's hard to explain," she began with a sigh. "It's about the Smiths. Have you met them?"

"Yes, I believe I have. I saddled horses for them yesterday."

"What do you think of them?"

Jack grinned. "Interesting family. I liked them. They're happy, cheerful, and they were wonderful folks through and through."

Anna sighed in disappointment. Jack didn't seem to understand her like she thought he would.

Jack saw Anna's face. "Why? What's wrong?"

"I don't really know how to say it, Jack," she replied with a long exhale. "I don't exactly feel comfortable around the Smiths, I guess. There's something strange about them all. I feel sorry for their youngest son, Colsson."

"Why is that?"

"He's so—" Anna paused and raised her troubled face to the sky, trying to find the words to say. "He's so terribly skinny."

Jack chuckled. "Is that all?"

"It's not funny, Jack. Have you seen him?"

Jack's face took on a puzzled frown. "Now that you mention it, I don't think so. I saddled an extra horse for another member of the family yesterday, but I didn't see him or her."

"You will change your mind when you see him," Anna stated firmly. She told him all the conversations she had had with Colsson and excluded nothing, not even finding the bloody sheets.

Jack stopped walking when she finished. "Anna." He turned her to face him and put his hand on her shoulder. "Your compassion is leading you in the wrong direction. All you can think of when you see him is him going through terrible things. Everything can be explained somehow. Don't let your feelings push you to imagining something that's not happening. Nothing's wrong. Understand?"

"My compassion is not the problem, Jack," said Anna. "Something is just not right. And if everything can be simply explained, why doesn't he tell me instead of avoiding certain things I ask him?"

The couple started walking again. "You *are* over-compassionate, sweetheart," he said. "You feel sorry for him being skinny and imagine all sorts of horrible things."

"Are you saying I shouldn't be compassionate?"

"I'm not saying that. It's good to be compassionate, but to be compassionate to the point of thinking something is wrong about some skinny guy when it's not, that's too much."

"What about the bloody sheets?"

A brief frown coated Jack's fair face. "Oh yeah, I forgot about that. Have you talked to anyone else about it?"

"My mom. She was going to talk to my dad about it. I don't think she has yet."

"Maybe he had a cut or two from something and didn't realize he was bleeding."

Anna bit her lip and thought. That would make sense, but… "What would the cuts be from?"

Jack shrugged. "That's for him to know and us not to, I guess."

Anna felt Jack's strong arm around her shoulders. She knew she could trust him. Peace flowed through her mind at the idea. A couple cuts? Whatever they were from they were most likely taken care of and under control now. She thought back to Colsson's reaction at seeing the sheets. He was simply embarrassed, that's all. Anna could have laughed at how silly her wild and worried thoughts had been over a couple accidental cuts. It was a perfectly simple thing that could have happened to anyone. So why had she been so confused? Why didn't that explanation come to her in the first place?

Jack and Anna walked together for a while longer. When they came to the gate where Emerald was standing, Jack asked, "Feeling better, sweetheart?"

Anna smiled at Jack. "I think so. Thank you, Jack."

He watched her climb onto the palomino. "Try not think about him today. Play volleyball, go swimming, go for a ride, and do anything so you don't think about him. Anytime you see him popping up in your mind, shove him out. Him being there tempts your imagination to think all kinds of things."

Anna nodded. "I'll try, Jack." She turned her horse to ride away.

The Smiths arrived after dinnertime as the sun was setting and displaying a mix of warm colors over the barnyard. Anna was going out the back door to see Jack when she saw Colsson on his hands and knees in the middle of the barnyard. Alarm filled her as she rushed toward the boy. "Colsson, are you alright?" she asked, trying to keep her fear inside. Not receiving an answer by the time she reached him, she put her hand on his shoulder.

Colsson let out a piercing yell and dropped the rest of the way to the ground. Anna gave a startled gasp and took a step back. Her heart beat wildly in her chest. She was completely unprepared for his scream. The boy lay still on the ground, eyes wide and mouth agape, breathing hard. What had happened?

"Dear Lord, please help him!" she prayed as she knelt next to him. "Colsson, are you okay?"

"No," Colsson whispered, his voice strangely hoarse. "Please, go away. Leave me here."

"Do you need help?" Anna asked, panic continuing to grow inside. She again whispered, "God, please help him!"

Colsson's anguish filled eyes changed to the cold, dreaded look Anna had seen once before. He shot up off the ground, a small but blood-chilling noise escaping his throat as he ran away, stumbling as he went. Anna ran after him. When she caught up to him, she turned to block his way.

"Colsson, what is wrong? How can I help you if I don't know what is troubling you?"

He lifted his face, which was now flushed a crimson red. "I don't need help," he sobbed. He pushed past her and kept going toward the house, walking this time, with his head down.

She remained where she stood and watched him go. More than anything, she wished she could simply understand what was wrong.

Up the stairs Colsson trudged with burdens growing heavier with each step. He stumbled into the room he shared with his brothers and collapsed in a heap near the window. His tears began afresh. His shoulders shook as sobs racked his body. "Why can't she understand that God has abandoned me? Why? Why? God doesn't care!"

Anna stood where she was for a long time. Her thoughts of confidence and peace she had felt after talking to Jack vanished. Apprehension, doubt, and an aching sensation crawled on her skin. Abruptly, she turned and went to the bunkhouse. She knocked on the rough wood door.

Jake responded to her knock. "Come in!"

Anna opened the door. Jake was alone, lying on his bed with his hands behind his head. Dirt streaks were on his face and arms, and his shirt torn from working with barbed wire. He pushed himself to a sitting position.

"Jake, do you know where Jack is?"

"Last time I saw him, he was in the barn. I think he was cleaning up some of the saddles."

"Thanks." She yanked the heavy door closed and ran to the barn. She forced herself to slow down when she reached it.

Jack was putting saddles away when Anna came in. Bits of straw were stuck in his hair. The smell of leather forever clinging to the tack room met her, though this time she hardly noticed it.

"Hi, Anna, what are you up to?" The muscles in his arms worked as he lifted another saddle and slung it up to a high rack.

Anna told him what had just happened a few minutes ago with Colsson. "There is something wrong, Jack, and it isn't my imagination."

"Sometimes people who don't believe in the Lord deal with a lot of anger and hurt," he said simply as he picked up another saddle.

"If that's all, then why was he on the ground and screaming like that?"

"That," Jack said as he pointed a finger at her, "is none of our business. Remember that."

Anna began to feel desperate. "If you were in here, how did you not hear him?"

"I think I heard something," Jack admitted. "I think he could have been startled when you came up to him."

Anna sighed in exasperation. What was the use? "I better go back inside," she said resignedly as she turned to leave.

Chapter Five

The next morning, Colsson wasn't at the dining table with the Smiths and the other guests. The family ate heartily while talking about their adventures the previous day. Anna frowned upon observing the empty chair. Not feeling well again, eh? She barely heard Saul and Esau talking wildly about a giant bass they'd hooked and battled to haul in.

As if someone knew the questions on Anna's tongue, one of the guests at the Smiths' table asked. "Where's your other boy?"

"He's extremely shy and doesn't like to come down all that much. Plus, he said he's not hungry this morning." Timothy didn't stop eating.

"Better get some meat on his bones, Timothy!" Another man chuckled and joked. "He's a real, live skeleton!"

The Smiths laughed with the rest, but for some reason, Anna felt like she had been slapped. How could they talk so lightly about Colsson? Yet, she also realized she wasn't the only one who noticed how dreadfully skinny he was. It was just a matter of how differently they thought of it from her. Something, something in the back of her mind about Colsson was bothering her still. What was it? Somehow, she felt as though she knew what was wrong, but she couldn't think of what it was.

After serving breakfast in the dining room, Anna went upstairs and knocked at the Smith boys' door.

"Come in," Colsson called.

As she opened the door, he rubbed his eyes and stared out the window. "Are you doing okay?"

"What do you want?" he asked in response.

"To make sure you're okay," Anna said gently. She felt her heart go out to the paper-thin creature standing by the window. She stood right behind him and put her hand on his shoulder.

He turned his tear-streaked face to look at her. "How can you lie like that? No one ever wants to be sure that I'm okay. No one cares."

"That's not true," Anna said softly. "I care. I'm not lying to you."

The crushed look of despair in his eyes lit slightly with hope. "You do?" he asked in quiet amazement. "How can that be?"

"Jesus asks us to."

Immediately his eyes grew cold.

Before he could say anything, however, Anna interjected, "God cares about you. More than I ever could."

Colsson's anger erupted. "How can you pretend that there is Someone who actually *likes* someone like me? How can you say that? You don't know what I've gone through! You don't know what it is to live your life unloved!"

Anna looked him in the eye. Strength swelled inside her. "You *think* you are unloved. You *believe* you are unloved. What you fail to understand is that you *are* loved."

He turned his face away. "*Love*," he scoffed. "What do you know of love?"

"Ask yourself the same question. You are ignorant of love. You don't know what love means because you refuse to see that you are loved more than you could ever know."

His jaw muscles moved, but he remained silent. He turned his head to see out the window again. The path of his eyes wandered far off into the distance, perhaps to a place she didn't know. She waited for a minute, and he finally choked out, "You can't understand."

Anna fought with herself. Maybe she really couldn't understand. Perhaps Colsson was not willing to tell her or anyone what was bothering him. "I was going to ask you to come with me to my secret place on the ranch today."

No answer. His lips moved slightly, like he would reply, but then he tightened them. He turned to look at her, and his lips moved again. That look was back. The same one that wanted to make her cry. Not a sound passed his lips. He looked back out the window.

Anna waited for a minute, then pressed, "Would you like to come?"

"No thanks," he said stiffly.

"May I ask why not?"

"I'd rather not say."

Anna took a step back, fighting to find the words to say. "Colsson—"

He interrupted her. "Let's just say this. My family would prefer I didn't."

Anna wrinkled her forehead in disbelief. Was he *still* governed by his family? She exhaled and nodded resignedly. "See you later." She left the room and quietly closed the door behind her. Quickly she made tracks for the kitchen where she knew her mother would be.

Liesel looked up from her work. "Is he still up there?"

"He's up there," Anna replied in an exasperated tone as she turned around in confused and exasperated circles. "What he's doing up there other than staring out the window, I don't know."

Liesel put her hand on her hip. "Anna," she said a little sharply. "Just let the boy alone." Her tone softened. "I talked to his parents and they said he likes to be by himself. He doesn't eat much very often, and they are trying to persuade him otherwise. So, you don't have to worry about him anymore."

"You talked to them? What did they say about the sheets?"

"He has a condition which causes him to bleed easily. They aren't sure, but they said he might have bumped the corner of a wall or something."

Relief filled Anna. "Now it's starting to make more sense."

Liesel gave her a smile. "I told you you didn't need to worry."

"There is one other thing, though. He refuses to understand that he's loved. He told me I don't know what it is to live my life unloved. And he is still under his family's control."

"How do you mean he is still under his family's control?"

"I asked him if he wanted to come to my place, and he said no. I think he does, but he said his family would prefer he didn't."

"You think everything he does or says is weird," Liesel said in a reproachful voice.

Anna lowered her voice to a serious tone. "Mom, if you saw the look in his eyes, you'd *know* something was wrong."

"Until I see it, honey, I'm not going to worry about it. I'll keep an eye out, I promise. I ask you not to worry either."

Anna sighed, closed her eyes, and bowed her head. "I will try, Mom. Somehow, I can't seem to shake it yet."

Liesel changed the subject. "Our breakfast is almost ready."

"I'm not very hungry this morning. If you don't mind, Mom, I'll skip. I might run down to my place."

"Go ahead, honey."

Anna closed the door behind her.

She cried aloud in rage as she rode Emerald to her place. Why couldn't her mother understand? She tried so hard to tell her mother something was wrong, but she wouldn't listen. "God, please help me," she prayed. "Help me understand what is happening. Help Mom, Dad, and Jack understand why I feel this way about Colsson. Show me the way. Is something wrong? Am I wrong in thinking what I have thought about him?"

The strange sense of peace that always came over her when her mind was troubled found her when the little meadow and grove of weeping willows came into view. Anna dismounted upon arrival and removed the lead rein from Emerald's halter like she always did. Tears of anger and frustration blinded her as she climbed the ladder to her treehouse. She closed the door behind her and sat down hard in the middle of the floor. She hugged her knees to her chest and rocked back and forth. Desperate prayers poured from her mind.

"BE STILL, AND WAIT FOR WHAT I HAVE PLANNED. I PROMISE YOU I WILL SHOW YOU WHAT I HAVE IN MIND IN MY GOOD TIME."

Instantly, Anna's troubled spirits left her, and peace swept over her. She lay on the floor and closed her eyes, exhaling peacefully.

Jack leaned on the rail of the fence and rubbed his eyes. He hadn't slept at all the previous night.

Jake walked up behind him and squeezed his younger brother's shoulder. "What's wrong? I heard you tossing and turning last night, and this morning you seem to be upset and tired."

Jack kept his head down, resting it on his wrists. "It's Anna."

Jake leaned on the fence, propping himself up on his elbow. "Want to talk about it?"

Jack lifted his head and gripped the rail. "I have a hard time understanding what she's feeling. I never really realized it before, but it's always been that way. Lately she's tried to talk to me about one of the guests, but it's difficult for me to understand her worries about it. It only ends up leaving her angry and frustrated."

"Have you talked to Mr. Campbell about it?"

Jack shook his head. "No. Not yet. I don't know what to do, Jake!"

"If there's only going to be anger, frustration, and trouble between you two now, you know as well as I do your marriage is not going to last. You want Anna to be happy, don't you?"

"Of course I do."

"Go find Mr. Campbell and talk to him."

Jack felt his brother's labor-roughened hand gently squeeze his shoulder, then heard Jake move away to return to his work. He stayed leaned over the fence, looking out over the pasture at the horses who were grazing without a care in the world. This was the hardest thing he'd ever had to do in his life. He loved Anna, but Jake was right. He knew their marriage wouldn't last. They couldn't be married without the element of understanding. Slowly, dread filling him to the fullest, he left the safety of the fence and went to find Frank.

The sober ranch hand walked into the barn, where Frank was working. Frank looked up to see Jack, concern crossing his face when their eyes met. "What's up, Jack?"

"Can I talk to you a minute, sir?"

Frank laid aside his pitchfork. "What's wrong?"

Jack choked and stumbled over his own words. He removed his hat and played with the rim, bending it nervously. "I was awake all night, and I came to realize that if Anna and I move forward with marriage, it won't last."

"What do you mean?"

"I have a hard time really listening and understanding her and talking to her. I try, but it doesn't seem to work. When she talks to me, I'm left with the feeling that I didn't help her at all, because I didn't know what she meant. It's always been that way, but just now do I realize that."

Frank nodded. "Being able to talk to each other is a very

important part of marriage. You are right in saying your marriage wouldn't last. I didn't know you two were having difficulty talking to each other. If I'd known, I would have talked to you about it sooner."

"What should I do?" Jack asked in a choked whisper.

Frank sighed sorrowfully. "For Anna's sake, you need to end it with her," he said gently.

"I wish you were in my place," Jack said miserably.

Frank exhaled. "Long ago, I *was* faced with the same situation. In high school, I had a girlfriend I had to break off with. It was the hardest thing to do, but in the end, I was glad I did. And you will be too, someday."

Jack bowed his head. Frank rested his hands on Jack's shoulders. "Go find Anna. You'd best talk to her now."

"I don't want to break her heart." Jack choked unexpectedly. Quickly he swallowed and brushed at his eyes, where tears were prompted by the sudden lump in his throat.

"Both of you may be brokenhearted, but this is what you need to do. And remember, you will still be friends."

Jack nodded and slowly turned to leave. His heart heavy, he mounted his horse. With no command to move forward, his horse stood still. Jack sat in silence, gazing at the path he had to take. The pain was unbearable.

Anna was still lying on the floor of the treehouse when she heard someone arrive. Crawling to the door, she looked down to see Jack. A smile lit her face, relief singing. He couldn't have arrived at a better time.

"Jack!" she exclaimed as she climbed down from the treehouse.

Jack's slow dismount instantly told her he did not share her joy. Her smile disappeared. "Jack, what's wrong?"

Jack kept his head down as he approached her. "I need to talk to you about something."

"About what?"

Jack lifted his face and shook his head. "It isn't of any use, Anna. I'm sorry."

"What do you mean? What isn't of any use?"

"You and me, Anna. We decided to court with the intention of marriage. Our marriage won't last, and I can't court you anymore. We can't be together like we have been."

Hurt shot down Anna's spine. "Jack, what do you mean?" she cried.

"We have a hard time talking to each other. We both know being able to talk to each other is essential. If we can't talk to each other and understand each other, our marriage will be useless." Jack's voice dropped to a choked whisper, and he looked her in the eye. "We can't go on together. I'm sorry." His throat moved as he swallowed. Anguish was written in his blue eyes as he drew her close.

Too shocked to say anything, Anna laid her head on Jack's chest. A silent lament filled her. Then, her thoughts told her, *"I won't ever marry the man I love."* Her tears fell through her shut lids, and she sobbed her heart out.

"I'm sorry," he whispered. His arms encased her tighter.

Anna couldn't say anything. Her heart torn in two, she sobbed uncontrollably. She didn't want any man from the outside world. She just wanted Jack.

Jack held onto Anna, rocking slightly from side to side. He rested his cheek against her head. Anna held close to Jack, keeping her cheek against his strong shoulder, and clutching his arm tightly.

Finally, Jack gently loosened her hold on him. The bright sun through the trees shone on his brown hair. He kissed her forehead and squeezed her hand. Slowly, he turned away. In silence he mounted his horse and rode away.

Anna watched silently, listening to the fading clip-clop of hooves. "God, why?" she wailed, gazing in the direction of Jack's departure. "I've lost the man dearest to me! I was so sure You wanted him to be my husband!"

"ANNA, I HAVE A GREATER PLAN IN MIND FOR YOU. BE STILL, AND WAIT."

Anna dropped to the ground in anguish. She wept with no control. For even with His comfort, she still struggled to overcome her sorrow, the likes of which she had never felt.

The sun touched the horizon, and a cool evening breeze slightly waved the long, drooping branches of the weeping willows. Anna still lay on the ground below her treehouse. Throughout the day, she had managed to control her tears, but whenever she remembered her broken dreams, smashed the moment Jack told her it wouldn't work between them, she cried again. Her head throbbed constantly.

Hooves approached, quietly thudding through the grass. Anna sat up and saw her father stopping his horse, Skylark. His eyes were full of sympathy.

"Jack talk to you?"

Anna nodded.

Frank dismounted and sat beside her. After a minute, he said, "Jack is a good man. I know he is, and I'd have proudly said yes if he'd one day asked for your hand in marriage. I'm truly sorry, honey. I've been there before. When I broke off with my girlfriend, I thought my life was done. I couldn't see how I could go on living. Till I met your mother. When I met your mother, my past thoughts changed. Your mother was better than anything and everything, even though I couldn't see how anything could be before I knew her. Trust me, it will be the same for you. I promise."

Tears kept falling down Anna's cheeks. Her voice quivered as she spoke. "How could anything be better than Jack?"

"That is *exactly* what I thought when I broke off with my girlfriend. But it became better. I have your mother, and we both have you."

"What if God doesn't intend things to be better for me like He did for you?"

Frank sighed. "Then He doesn't. But He works all things out for the good of those who love Him. Do you remember Jeremiah 29:11? *'For I know the thoughts that I have thought towards you, saith the Lord, even the thoughts of peace, and not of trouble, to give you an end, and your hope.'"* Frank rose and offered his hand to help her up. "Let's go home, Anna."

Anna took his hand and got up. She whistled for her mare. Emerald tossed her head from where she was grazing across the brook and came to Anna. The two of them mounted their horses and turned them toward the main ranch.

Liesel was waiting in the kitchen when Anna and Frank came in. "Anna, you had me worried all day," she scolded. "You haven't eaten anything."

Anna made no reply but kept her eyes on the floor.

"Liesel," said Frank. He signaled her to come close to him.

Anna slowly walked to the table, sat down, and buried her head in her arms.

Liesel stepped past her daughter and asked Frank, "What's up with her?"

Frank took Liesel by the arm and guided her to the laundry room. He bent closer to her and said quietly, "Jack broke it off with her this morning. He decided he'd best not court her anymore, and I believe he made a wise decision in doing so."

Liesel's mouth dropped open. "Jack broke it off with her? Why?"

"He talked to me before talking to her. He explained he was having a conflict because he and Anna have a hard time talking to and understanding each other. I told him, and he knew, the best thing to do for both of their sakes was to end it with her."

"And he did?"

"He went out to her treehouse and told her. He's just as heartbroken as she is. I saw him when he got back. It will take time, but in the end, they will both come to realize that this was the right thing to do."

"I never realized that they were having such a hard time understanding each other," Liesel whispered sadly in disbelief.

"It's mostly him who is having the difficult time, which makes it all the harder for her."

Liesel sighed and gazed sorrowfully at Anna after she and Frank left the laundry room. "Dinner is ready," she said after a minute.

Anna was empty on the inside. Too disturbed to eat, her dinner went untouched. She went to bed a little later and cried herself to sleep.

In the bunkhouse, a heartbroken Jack tossed and turned, trying to sleep and wishing the events of the day were only a nightmare. No matter how hard he tried, sleep wouldn't come...wouldn't come...wouldn't come. He too was empty on the inside. How could he have hurt the woman he loved?

Jake's snores seemed louder than normal. To Jack, the consistent, quiet noise was an annoyance. He rolled onto his side and pulled the sheets farther over his shoulders. A quiet tear slipped down his face, hung onto his nose, and dripped with a soft thud onto the cotton sheet. More followed. In an effort to keep them from falling, he squeezed his eyes shut and clenched his teeth. No use. He gave up the fight, but the tears relented little.

"God help me," he prayed as he tossed and turned. "If You are willing, bring us back together."

"I HAVE A GREATER PLAN IN MIND," God whispered. "TRUST ME."

Finally, simply with the sound of God's quiet and calm voice, Jack fell asleep.

Chapter Six

Colsson felt as sober as Anna looked the next morning at the table. His parents and brothers laughed and talked to the other guests while he sat silently. When Anna came to serve him, she asked the usual question, "How much do you want?"

"I'm not hungry," he forced himself to say.

Exasperation came into Anna's eyes. Visibly she was tired of this response. "Well gosh darn it, you've got to eat something sometime!" she said in a hushed voice. "You're going to starve to death one of these days."

Colsson snapped his head around and with a glare, he dared her to say it again. How could she?

Anna's own troubles vanished in an instant. Why was he acting this way? Instinct told her to immediately tell her parents, but, remembering her parents' firm beliefs about the Smith family, she abandoned this idea. There was something in Colsson's eyes that revealed she had hit the truth, but in an indirect way. What was happening?

"Do you want to come to my treehouse today?" she asked him in a low voice, being careful not to let anyone else hear her.

Colsson gave a sigh, looked at his empty plate, and nodded.

"Right after breakfast, I'll meet you in the barnyard." Anna left and went to the other table.

Colsson twisted his head around and watched Anna's back. Should he tell her?

Anna waited in the barnyard. Where was Colsson? Breakfast had ended half an hour ago. His family had already left.

Anna heard a whisper from behind her.

"Anna! Anna!"

Startled, she wheeled sharply and saw Colsson inside the barn. She jogged toward him. "What are you doing in there?"

Colsson didn't answer. "How far away is it?"

"Not far, but a long walk on foot. I'll take you on horseback."

Anna retrieved two lead reins and halters and started walking toward the pasture where her mare was grazing. She stopped when she realized Colsson wasn't following her. Like a shy little colt, he stayed in the shadows inside the barn. She went back. "Colsson, don't you want to come?"

He nodded.

"Why are you hiding?"

Colsson's usual silence reigned. His gaze flitted briefly to the third floor of the ranch house.

The desire to be a good friend surged through her. She drew closer. "Colsson," she said softly. "You don't have to be afraid."

Colsson bowed his head. "You don't understand. I don't think I should have come."

Anna didn't even think, and words came out. "Colsson, I promise, you are safe. If anything ever happens, my father and the ranch hands will protect you."

The muscles in his thin cheeks worked as he wrestled with himself. His hands shook, and he gripped the barn door jamb until his knuckles turned white. A new look filled his eyes: a fight for strength.

Anna took his hand and led him across the barnyard to the pasture. When she had closed the gate behind them, she pointed to a quarter horse gelding near Emerald. "You can ride that horse there. His name's Butterscotch." She put the halter on the gelding. "You can talk to him for a bit while I get Emerald."

With the same gentleness he had used before with Emerald, Colsson drew near Butterscotch and began to stroke the horse's face. When Anna had tied the lead rein onto her mare, she stood watching Colsson and Butterscotch for a minute. Colsson seemed to gain a new courage and confidence as he softly stroked Butterscotch's coat.

After Anna led them out of the pasture and closed the gate, she showed Colsson how to mount bareback. After several tries, Colsson managed to climb aboard Butterscotch. Anna mounted Emerald and nudged her to a walk toward her treehouse.

Colsson tapped his heels against Butterscotch's sides.

The mysterious silence which often governed Colsson returned. He rode in silence, as though lost in thought.

Anna turned around to see Colsson. He kept his eyes down and barely even moved. Anna sighed and turned back to face ahead. Memories of the previous day popped into her mind, and tears filled her eyes. Returning to the place where her heart had been broken so violently was almost unbearable. Tears blurring her vision, she turned again to gaze softly at Colsson. Perhaps he was suffering from heartbreak just as she was. Her lip trembled, and she silently vowed to be there for him in every way she could.

When they reached the treehouse, Colsson lifted his eyes, and when he saw the quiet beauty, he felt his burdens lift from his shoulders. He gazed all around him in wonder. How could any place like this exist? The willows' branches softly touched the grass, the birds chirped, the sunlight filtered through the trees, and the quiet beauty of this place chased away all his fears. He now felt at peace, truly at peace. He hardly noticed Anna dismount.

Slowly, he slid off Butterscotch, staring at the branches above him. Sunlight covered his legs with golden stripes and warmed his blond hair. He turned to take in the brook and the meadow beyond.

Anna took the lead reins from both horses and slapped their rumps to encourage them across the brook. She gazed at Colsson after the horses left. Instead of the fearful, strange silence always presiding, this was a new silence, a peaceful silence.

Colsson sat down at the base of the tree beneath Anna's treehouse and slowly eased himself against the trunk. He laid his head back. The stripes of sunlight now covered his whole body. He closed his eyes. Anna sat beside him without a word. She dared not disturb this new peace he needed so much.

A few minutes later, he opened his eyes and said, "This is the first bit of happiness I've ever had. I've heard talk of happiness, but never understood until now. This is the first time it's ever felt real to me."

"You've been unhappy in your life," Anna whispered. "That much I know just by being around you."

"Please tell me the meaning of friend," he said quietly.

"A friend is someone who will share your happiness and your sadness. Laughs with you and cries with you. Understands your hardships and does everything in their power to help you. A friend will always be there for you no matter what happens. A friend will walk with you in the good times, and let you cry on their shoulder during the bad times."

"Friend," he whispered. "Friend." He closed his eyes again.

"Why do you ask?"

His eyelids opened once more. "You are the only friend I've ever had, Anna. I wish I never had to leave here."

"Colsson, something has not been right, and I have been yearning to find out what is troubling you for the sake of helping you. What's wrong?"

Colsson leaned forward stiffly, groaning as he did so. "I've never told anyone what I feel I should tell you. I don't know what will happen to me."

Anna said nothing and waited. She offered up a silent prayer for guidance for his decisions.

"If anyone found out I told you..." Colsson's voice trailed off, leaving the sentence unfinished.

"What do you mean?" asked Anna, a tiny tingle creeping down her spine.

"My family, who most people think of as some of the nicest people in the world, really isn't."

A thought struck Anna. "They don't *starve* you, do they?" she breathed the words in disbelief.

He exhaled and nodded. "Yes. They do."

"That's why I have found you in your room, and you've said you weren't hungry. You were, but you were—"

"Forced to say that," he finished. "I won't go into detail as to what would happen if I don't, but it is an awful thing."

"And this is why you say you aren't loved."

"That's the truth."

"In time you'll come to realize you *are* loved," Anna said gently.

A saddened look came into his eyes, and she knew he still didn't believe her. She sighed and after a moment of silence, spoke again. "How long have these things been happening to you?"

"I feel like I have been dealing with this my whole life but yet, not quite. I don't remember anything from my childhood. They never talk about when I was a little boy. I can't imagine what it was like."

Anna cocked her head. "That's really odd. Most people can remember at least some things from their childhood."

Colsson shrugged and picked at the grass.

"They abuse you, and you never tell anyone?" she pressed.

He shrugged again. "Till now."

"Don't you realize that if you had told somebody sooner you wouldn't be suffering like this?"

"I don't have anybody to tell," he said simply.

"Colsson, if your family is abusing you, you need to tell the law enforcement. They can intercede, and you won't have to be with them any longer."

His head jerked up, plainly startled. "Law enforcement? I've heard about that. My family has told me if I ever talk to law enforcement, or anyone for that matter, they would..." His voice broke off.

Fear swelling, she pushed past her dry lips, "They would what?"

"Kill me." His voice was a whisper and his jaw tight.

"Kill you?" She gave a little shriek. "They wouldn't do that!"

"They're dead serious," he said bitterly. "Every now and then they make things even worse for me to make sure I understand that. If they found out I told you, they'd—"

"You mean you are risking your life to tell me," Anna concluded, speaking more to herself than him.

"That's pretty much it."

"My family will keep you safe," she said gently. "They only need know what you're going through."

He hesitated, shuddering at the thought of the consequences. Should he really take this chance? "You can tell them, but do it quietly so my family will not know."

"I promise I will do my best." A heavy burden lifted from her shoulders. Ready to take action, Anna squeezed his shoulder.

"Are you feeling better now that you have told me the truth

instead of hiding it from everyone?"

He nodded slowly. "In a way, but still, perhaps I shouldn't have."

"You did the right thing, Colsson. I pray your hardships will come to an end because you did."

Colsson hugged his bony knees to his chest, releasing a long exhale. Deep down, he desperately hoped Anna was right. Still, he wrestled with the feeling of dread. He ached with the feeling that his family somehow already knew.

Anna put her arms around him and hugged him. "It'll be okay, Colsson, I promise."

"I feel it never will be," he began as he rested his head on her shoulder.

Anna laid a quiet finger on his lips. "Please do not speak of it anymore now. I'm here."

In the warmth of Anna's arms, Colsson felt no desire to move. He closed his eyes and let her chase away his fear. He rested a hand on her leg.

After letting him go, Anna stood and said, "I'll take you back, and you can eat with our family. We can talk to them then."

"No, please!" he gasped. "I can't do that! If my family found out I was eating with your family..."

"What do you mean? How could they find out you ate with us? You aren't worried about being here."

"They left after breakfast, but they're coming back around lunch time. I had better be back before they are, for the sake of not letting on that anything has happened. They locked the door as usual, but I wasn't in there. They thought I had been. That's the only reason I made it here. I was worried I couldn't."

Anna squeezed his shoulder. "Let's go back."

Colsson slowly pushed himself to his feet. His legs shook as though it took all of his strength to get up. When he finally managed to stand, he staggered and put his hand to his head. He fell back against the tree trunk and would have fallen to the ground if Anna hadn't rushed to his side and put her arm around his waist to support him.

"Colsson, are you okay?"

"Dizzy," he murmured as he put his arm around her shoulder and relied on her for support. "I couldn't see anything for a minute, and I nearly lost my balance. That happens to me a lot."

"That's because you haven't eaten anything today. You okay now?"

He nodded. "Yeah, I think so."

Anna collected the horses and tied the lead reins onto their halters. She led Butterscotch to Colsson. He was still a little dizzy.

"Can you mount? I can help you get up."

He didn't reply, but took the reins, put them over the gelding's head, and managed to mount by himself after a couple tries. "I'm used to this. I'll be fine." He gazed down at Anna and gave her a soft smile.

Anna mounted got on Emerald and led the way back toward the main ranch.

"When is lunch?" Colsson asked suddenly. A slight burst of panic seized him.

"Not for another couple hours," Anna replied. "We only finished breakfast a short while ago. You and I haven't been gone that long."

"Still, let's get back fast," he said anxiously.

Anna nudged Emerald to a trot. "Give Butterscotch a little kick, and he'll go faster," she called back to him.

Colsson did so, and Butterscotch readily responded.

When they entered the barnyard, they stopped their horses

next to the pasture gate and dismounted. They took the halters off and let the horses out to graze with the others.

While Anna's back was turned, Colsson put his hand to his back which seemed strangely sweaty for only horseback riding. He took one look at his hand, and his eyes widened. Quickly he scooped up dust in his hand, rubbed his hands together, and let the dust fall back to the ground.

His legs shook slightly, and he shivered. Behind him, he sensed Anna's arm nearing him to support him. Before she could touch him, he quickly raised his hand and lifted his arm, twisted slightly, and blocked her arm. "Please don't," he murmured.

"I saw you shake and worried you might go down again."

He kept his arm up. "I know. Please, don't touch me for now."

"What is it?"

"Hard to explain." Colsson slowly lowered his arm.

"What would you like to do now?" she asked although she was sure of the answer.

"I'd best go up to my room until my family gets back so they won't suspect anything."

"Colsson, are you sure?" she asked, not expecting this reply. "I think you better eat while you can."

He shook his head. "I can't risk it. I don't know exactly when they'll be back."

Anna stood in front of him and looked him in the eye. "You *will* starve to death if you let yourself."

He looked at the ground and bit his lip.

"Come on," she said gently. "I'll see what I can find."

He followed Anna to the ranch house. She led him into the dining room, and he reluctantly sat down. Anna went to the kitchen. Liesel wasn't there. She looked in the refrigerator and found a few breakfast leftovers. She decided against heating them up in order to get them out to Colsson as quickly as possible. Almost before she set them down, he was eating as quickly as he could from starvation.

Anna went back to the kitchen and washed dishes while he ate. When she went back to check on him, she was met with an empty dining room. He was gone! Some of his food was still there, and his fork was on the floor. "Colsson?" Anna called alarm ripping through her like a bullet. She dropped her dishtowel on the table and raced up the stairs to the third floor.

Without thinking, she rapped on the Smith boys' room door. Saul opened it. Anna's mouth gaped. "Hi, when did you guys get back?" she babbled.

"Just a little bit ago," Saul said cheerfully. "You look like you've seen a ghost. Did you need something?"

"I was looking for something." The words rolled off her tongue. "May I come in?"

Saul stood to the side. "Of course."

Anna entered and pretended to search for something. Colsson was sitting under the window on the floor in the room, resting his arms on his bent knees. He fidgeted with his fingers and didn't look up when Anna came in. Had his family taken him away from the table and brought him up here? One look at him told her that was probably the case.

"I guess it's not here," Anna said. "Thank you for letting me look."

"Anytime," Saul said as he shut the door behind her.

As Anna walked away, all she could think was, *How can he act like that? How can he be so casual as though nothing were out of the ordinary? They took Colsson from something he needed so much. I have to talk to Mom and Dad about this. And Jack—*

Then she remembered. Jack was no longer someone to whom she could go. He was easy for her to talk to, but he didn't understand how or why she felt certain ways. He didn't seem to know how to help her, even though he listened.

Remembering this drained Anna completely, leaving her feeling empty inside. Loneliness crept over her. She sank down on the stairs and hid her face in her hand. "God help me," she whispered.

After sitting on the stairs for several minutes, she somehow found the strength to rise and go back to the kitchen. Her mother still hadn't returned, so she began lunch for the boarders. Not long after she started, Liesel came in from working outside. She hung her sunhat on a hook in the washroom and came to help Anna in the kitchen.

"Mom, I have something I need to tell you," Anna began.

"If it's about Colsson, I don't want to hear it." Liesel said. She slammed her knife down through a potato.

"Please, Mom, this is important. I need to tell you this and when I do, you'll understand."

Liesel held up her hand. "I said I don't want to hear it, and I meant it, Anna."

Anna tightened her lips and silently went back to her work. She prayed silently as she cut celery. "How long, oh Lord? Must Colsson suffer forever? Please help Mom understand that something really *is* wrong."

"ANNA, TRUST ME. I AM DOING EVERYTHING ACCORDING TO MY PLAN. KEEP TRYING AND DON'T GIVE UP."

Dad, Anna thought. *I will try to talk to Dad at lunch. Maybe then they'll both listen to me.*

Impatiently, Anna helped Liesel as she waited for her father to come in. Why was it at times like these, the person she wanted to talk to immediately was never around?

When lunch was ready, Frank finally came in. Anna waited, her legs tense, until he had prayed, then she said, "Dad, something *is* wrong with Colsson."

Liesel narrowed her eyes and said firmly, "Anna, no."

"Your mother talked to me about this, Anna," said Frank. "And she's right. The Smiths are wonderful people, as is everybody here. You yourself know we make absolutely sure we don't get a boarder that isn't safe to have here."

"Dad, you and Mom don't understand," she pleaded although she knew it was futile.

"Anna, it's okay," said Frank. "I promise."

Frank and Liesel began talking to each other about other subjects. Anna pushed her full plate away, hoping Liesel would ask why she wasn't hungry. Then she would reply, *"If Colsson can't eat, neither will I."*

While waiting for the expected question, Anna prayed, "God, what should I do? Why don't my parents trust me?"

"THEY WILL IN TIME. IT WILL COME SUDDENLY. LET ME GUIDE YOU TO THE WORDS TO SAY, ACCORDING TO MY WILL. I PROMISE, GOOD WILL COME OF ALL THIS."

Anna let go of her impatience and pulled her plate back in front of her.

Chapter Seven

Anna took Colsson to the treehouse periodically over the next days, armed with food for him to eat. When there, Colsson was no longer the shy little shadow she'd previously known. It was as though he had completely changed. He was happy and acted as though he was no longer under someone's control. He walked strongly, talked strongly, and even laughed. When Anna told him a funny story about when she was younger, he threw his head back laughing.

Anna smiled as she walked and listened to someone she never thought could laugh. He had such a wonderful laugh. And it seemed as though their friendship was growing deeper by the day. He had no stories from his childhood to tell her in exchange, but he talked freely. Anna left her heartbreak behind as she walked and talked to him.

One day, after walking through the meadow in silence, Anna felt Colsson's fingertips brush against her arm, and then they slipped into her hand. He held her hand gently and moved closer to her. Anna felt rather awkward. Only Jack had ever held her hand this way. She didn't want to let go, though. *Perhaps he doesn't really realize what he is doing. Maybe it's okay. We <u>are</u> friends, and maybe he just needs to feel a little closer.*

"We should come here tomorrow too," said Anna with a smile several minutes later.

"I don't think tomorrow will work, Anna," Colsson replied sorrowfully. "My family is going on an all-day trip and taking me with them. It's going to be rough. There are still some things I haven't told you, and I won't until it's all over."

"I've tried to talk to my parents about it, but they don't really seem to believe that anything is wrong. I'm so sorry."

He sighed. "I know it isn't your fault. I'm just tired of suffering. For once I'd like to live my life unafraid." He spread out his free arm. "As I am here."

Anna nodded, and pride and love for this place swelled inside her. "When you are tired, longing to get away, this is the place to come."

"I'm glad to have you for a friend, Anna. You're the first one I've ever had in my life. Coming here has introduced me to many things I had never understood before."

"I'm glad to have you for a friend too, Colsson. You've changed since coming here."

"I know I have," he agreed. He turned around to face her and walked backward. "When I first came here, I wouldn't have talked to you like I am talking to you now."

"Just look at you," Anna said with a chuckle. "You're actually acting like a man instead of a terrorized little boy."

He smiled and turned back around to walk next to her. "You remember that dance going on the day we arrived?"

"Yeah?"

"Well, I was kept from coming."

"Saul said you wouldn't come because you were so shy."

"That might have been partially true. But mostly, Saul said that to cover up the fact that they were forcing me to keep away from people who might figure out what's really happening."

"Oh." Things clicked in Anna's mind. It was all beginning to make sense.

"Is there going to be another dance sometime?"

"I don't know. That would be a question for my parents."

"I'd sure like to give that dancing thing a try. I'd like to learn how."

"I'll let you know if we decide to do another dance," she promised. She changed the subject. "We probably better head back, Colsson. We've been here for several hours."

"What time is it?" he asked in alarm. "My family doesn't know about any of this. If they find out someone unlocked the door and let me out—"

"They shouldn't be back for a long time. You never know, but still. At least you got to come here and eat for once."

"Yes," he murmured gratefully. "Thank you for that."

Anna smiled at him, relieved he had the chance to turn away from the ill-treatment always following him. "You're welcome."

"I guess we better get home so you can lock me in my room before my family gets back," he said with a wry smile.

Anna didn't say anything, sorrowful this time had come to an end. Colsson had changed! No longer was he so afraid of even her. Before, her every sudden move had startled him, but it didn't anymore as he'd learned to trust her and know she wouldn't hurt him.

The ride back was all too short. Not much was said, each dreading the time to part, and each fearing the things that could possibly happen while they were apart. They paused outside the Smith boys' room door. Anna unlocked the door and opened it.

Before going in, however, Colsson said, "Thank you, Anna."

"You're welcome, Colsson," she replied, hardly hearing herself speak as she gazed deep into his blue-green eyes.

He put his arms around her and hugged her tightly. When he let her go, he gave a warm smile and murmured, "My first real hug." He stroked a lock of Anna's hair resting against her shoulder and disappeared inside his room. She closed the door and locked it again, then she slowly walked downstairs.

Late that night, she remembered back to her time she had had with him earlier that day. How wonderful it had been! How easily she could put her heartbreak behind her when she was with him.

While turning this over in her mind, she suddenly came to realize she had come to care very much about Colsson. A tingle went up and down her spine; the same one she had when she began to care about Jack. She closed her eyes and briefly imagined Colsson as her husband. She opened her eyes again. Could it be? Could she be learning to care about him as more than a friend?

Immediately she was met with conflicts. He wasn't a Christian. And the thought of the Smiths being her in-laws made her want to throw up. Fear struck her for any children she and Colsson might have. If the Smiths got their hands on the children...

"Hold off, hold off!" Anna murmured aloud. "It's the guy who has to make the first move. Marriage will never even cross his mind."

Little did Anna know, she was wrong. Colsson sat by the window, looking out at the moon as his brothers snored in bed. "I want to be with her forever," he whispered softly. "Is there any way? If only I could. I want to be with her every waking moment. I feel I can't live without her."

Peace filled him as though there were a way he could have his greatest wish. Hope for the future surged through him. Hope his suffering would end. Hope that he could have a wonderful life after all. With Anna.

The hope and peace were suddenly torn from him. He knew his family would force him to return with them. He felt sure they would rather kill him than run the risk of people finding out their way of handling him. They weren't going to let him go. Not for the world. A lonely tear trickled down his cheek.

Why did he have to remember that Anna might not be able to save him from his long suffering? The Smiths didn't have much time left at the ranch. How long was it? A week? Two weeks?

It *can still happen,* he thought. He rested his arms on the windowsill. Hope filled him again, and the newly found feeling of happiness warmed him through.

Colsson awoke abruptly from sleeping when someone grabbed his shoulder and shook him violently. His eyes flew open and he uttered a little cry.

"Come on," said Saul gruffly. "We've got to get going."

He groaned and struggled to push himself up on his hands and knees.

"I said get up!" Saul shouted. He reached down and shoved Colsson over.

Colsson cried again. As he tried to get up, a shadow fell over him. "Saul, no!" He abandoned hopes of getting up in time. He held up his arm to shield himself, and looked away, squeezing his eyes shut and clenching his teeth.

Saul kicked him in the gut, hard as he could. Colsson emitted a frightening howl of agony and writhed on the floor, moaning loudly. He rolled himself into a tight ball, trying to ease the pain in his gut.

The door to the room was wrenched open. "Keep the noise down!" Timothy hissed, eyes narrow. "You're going to alert the entire ranch!" He rushed over to Colsson and clamped a brutal hand over the boy's mouth.

Tears squeezed through Colsson's closed eyelids. A muffled sob in his throat, barely audible even to him, pushed its way through Timothy's hand.

Someone knocked on the door. Timothy quickly yanked and dragged Colsson into the bathroom, still not allowing him to make a sound. Colsson heard one of his brothers open the door.

"Is everything alright?" a male voice asked. "My wife and I thought we heard something a few minutes ago."

"Everything's okay," Esau replied. "My twin brother stubbed his toe a good one."

"Okay," the voice said with relief in his tone. "Where's your other brother? Will he be able to come down this morning?"

Colsson squirmed slightly. He was tempted to kick Timothy, but thought better of it. The consequences if he did that were too great to risk. Still, his legs tingled with the temptation.

"He's actually doing well this morning, so we're all going on an all-day ride into the back country and taking him with us. We're leaving before breakfast is ready."

"I'm glad he's doing better," said the man. "Hopefully you'll be able to do more things together as a family. That must be miserable for him to be stuck here all day."

"It is," Esau replied.

"You have a good day," said the man. "Safe travels!"

"Thanks," replied Esau. The door closed, and Colsson heard Esau blow air from his cheeks.

Timothy shoved Colsson out the bathroom door. He fell to the floor, gasping for breath. Timothy made his way toward the door. "Be ready to leave in ten minutes."

Colsson breathed heavily. As soon as the door was closed behind Timothy, he closed his eyes and let his head fall to the floor with a moan.

Saul crossed the room and yanked him to his feet. Colsson gave a weak little cry of pain. "Get dressed."

Colsson forced himself to rise move toward the dresser. Bit by bit, the pain in his gut ebbed away.

About ten minutes later, Timothy rapped on the boys' door. Colsson's heart skipped a beat. The time had come.

"Ready, Dad!" called Esau as he struggled to finish the top

82

button of his shirt. He turned to the others. "Come on, let's go!"

Colsson found himself in between Esau and Saul on the way down the stairs. He walked quietly, but his fingers tingled with terror over what he knew would probably be happening that day. Dread filled him to the fullest, he walked numbly, and he ached with despair. There would be no use begging, pleading, or trying any other way to stay behind. *I'd rather have been left in my room to starve.* These words echoed over and over in his mind.

"PRAY," came the soft reply.

No! He tossed his head and held it high, clenching his jaw. *God has never helped me in the past, why would now be any different? I will never go back! Never!*

"HAVE FAITH. YOU LACK FAITH."

If You cared, why do you not hear me? Why have You allowed me to suffer as I do? he silently challenged in return. *You don't care!* With that, he closed off any other reply from the Lord.

"Mornin'," said Jack when he met up with the Smiths in the barnyard. "Horses are ready to go."

Colsson observed Jack. To his great surprise, Jack looked rather sad, and somewhat like he felt: crushed, despairing. For a brief moment, the dread lifted from his shoulders, and he no longer felt alone. When they began walking again, however, it returned.

"Thanks," said Timothy as he followed Jack.

All was still in the early morning. The barnyard was silent and glowed a dull yellow from the morning sun. Jack led the Smiths to the corral where the horses were waiting.

"Oh!" cried Polly. "I almost forgot! I have to run back to the house. Mrs. Campbell said she'd leave a picnic lunch for us on the dining room table."

Polly went back to retrieve the almost-forgotten package.

Colsson waited on edge until she came back, and they all mounted their horses. Timothy led them out on a barely visible path toward the north. The path wound its way through rolling country of small hills, tiny meadows, and into the timbered hills beyond.

Several miles from the main ranch, they came to a gate set in the fence. Timothy stopped his horse, dismounted, and opened the gate.

"Um, Dad?" said Esau, leaning forward in his saddle. "That isn't private land, is it?"

"Nope," Timothy replied. "I found out from the cowboys."

"Are we allowed to go there?"

"Nobody said we could, nobody said we couldn't," said Timothy as he remounted. He twisted in the saddle to look at Esau. "You got cold feet?"

Esau shook his head vigorously. "Nope!"

"Let's go, then," said Timothy. "But Colsson, here you walk."

Colsson felt the color drain from his face. Before he could say anything, Timothy yelled, "Move!"

Slowly, reluctantly, he swung his leg over the cantle and stepped down to the ground. He clutched the reins in his hand, wishing he had the guts to stay on the horse and high tail it back to the main ranch. Why not? They didn't know he knew how to ride. They probably thought he was just hanging on without a clue as to guiding a horse.

"Saul, lead his horse."

Saul immediately reached over and took the horse's reins.

Colsson's vision blurred, and he clenched his fists as the group began to move again. Through his tears, he caught sight of Polly giving him a sympathetic look.

"I can't, I can't, I can't," Colsson kept saying to himself as he struggled to keep up with the horses and battle the rough ground. Tears dripped down his nose. With every step, he wished he had made for the main ranch.

The journey seemed endless. For hours, he had plodded on with his head down. He lifted his head and saw Timothy's back. Hate burst through him.

I *hate you!* He screamed inwardly. He paused his walking. Tears were racing down his cheeks in raging streams now. He grit his teeth in anger. He fell forward to his knees and supported himself on his hands.

"I can't go on anymore!" he shrieked.

The rest of the family stopped their horses and turned around to face him.

Colsson looked up at Timothy. "I hate you!" he cried. He pounded his fist into the dirt. "I *hate* you!"

Saul and Esau began to dismount.

"No," said Timothy. "Stay where you are. *I'm* going after him." He dismounted and strode quickly toward Colsson.

Strengthened by the torrent of hate in his soul, Colsson leaped to his feet and sprinted away from Timothy. Timothy ran after him, and quickly overtook the young man. He grabbed Colsson by the shoulders and yanked him down to the ground.

Colsson got back up again, but before he could go anywhere, Timothy punched him in the jaw, sending him flying back to the ground. He reached down, hauled Colsson to his feet again and bashed the thin youth against a tree. As an added measure of cruelty, he clamped his large hand over Colsson's throat.

Colsson began to choke.

"*You have been warned,*" Timothy growled in a low, threatening tone. Sweat poured down his face and he breathed heavily as his face drew near to Colsson's. "You have been warned what would happen if you defied me."

Polly clutched the horn of her saddle until her hands turned white. Her eyes were closed, and she scarcely breathed, as she struggled to decide. Timothy's warnings to her to not interfere haunted her. Colsson's choking sounds filled her ears. She knew Timothy wouldn't kill him, but he couldn't breathe! Why, how, could Timothy be so cruel?

"Timothy! Stop it!" Polly screamed. Her eyes flew open.

Startled, Timothy released his grip on his son.

Colsson fell to the ground, choking and drawing in air. He lay still, struggling to breathe. Blood slowly trickled from his lip.

Timothy moved toward Polly. "Polly!" he said in the same threatening tone. Then he raised his voice. "Polly!"

"I...I had to say something," Polly whispered. "I couldn't bear it."

Timothy stood next to Polly's horse. He let out a war cry and reached up to pull Polly off her horse.

"Dad, he'll try to get away again!" said Saul.

Timothy stopped where he was. He looked from Colsson back to Polly. "Don't, *ever,* do it again. First he accepts the girl's help, then pulls this stunt. We should have gotten him out here a lot sooner."

Timothy marched back to Colsson and jerked him upright.

Saul reached into his saddlebags and removed a length of rope. He tossed it to Timothy.

Timothy crossed Colsson's wrists in front of him and tied them together, then wrapped the end of the rope around the horn of his saddle and tied it off. "Let's see you try that episode again," he sneered after he mounted.

Colsson said nothing in reply. His head was down in defeat. When the group started again, he was forced to keep up with the pace of Timothy's horse. Although he had a fair amount of slack, the rope constantly went taut, threatening to pull him over completely. Slight sobbing sounds escaped his throat as he stumbled blindly along.

It seemed like hours before they reached a small ring in the midst of the timber where there were no trees. The grass was short, but the same kind in the meadows they had left behind them so long ago. No rocks were in it, and it was level. Out-reaching branches of the surrounding trees shaded them.

When they halted, Esau reached over out of his saddle to untie Colsson's hands. Once released, he fell to his hands and knees. He sat back on his heels to relieve the pressure from his hands and wrists.

Colsson's sobs had slowed to tiny hiccupping. He closed his eyes and lifted his face toward the sky. Blood from his lip had dried. An occasional tear still leaked from his closed eyelids. Exhaustion and defeat tore at him. When? When would this end? Why couldn't it be done? He had been suffering for so long!

"PRAY," came the Voice again. "PRAY, AND BELIEVE."

"No," he whispered. "It's not true! He's never helped me in the past. Why would He help me now?"

"HAVE YOU DISREGARDED EVERYTHING ANNA HAS TOLD YOU ABOUT LOVE? HAVE YOU NOT LISTENED? IGNORANT BOY!"

Colsson felt as though he had been struck. Yet, that hate poured into his heart again. *I hate You! There is nothing You can do to bring me to You! I will never give in. You cannot fool me with talk of love. Not when I know You do not love me!*

"IN THE END, YOU WOULD HAVE REGRETTED THOSE WORDS WITH ALL YOUR SOUL. WILL YOU NOT RETURN TO ME?"

Why don't You figure it out?

"I KNOW WHAT WILL HAPPEN. I HAVE PLANNED EVERYTHING TO THE END."

Please! Please leave me alone!

"KNOW THAT I WILL NEVER BE SILENCED. THERE IS NOTHING YOU SAY THAT WILL COMMAND ME TO BE STILL. I ALONE HAVE CONTROL OVER

THAT. I HAVE CONTROL OVER EVERYTHING, EVEN YOU, EVEN THE FAMILY THAT SO CRUELLY TREATS YOU WITHOUT LOVE. I AM NOT LIKE THAT."

You are worse than they are to leave me struggling under them! How can You claim to love me, but don't care enough to help me from this?

"THE TIME HAS NOT COME FOR THE PAIN TO END. BUT I PROMISE, I WILL NEVER LEAVE YOU NOR FORSAKE YOU. ALL I WANT IS TO BE YOUR FRIEND."

I *will never be Your friend! How ridiculous would it be for someone to be friends with a voice in the shadows?*

"I AM NOT MERELY A VOICE IN THE SHADOWS. I AM THE BEGINNING AND THE END, THE ALPHA AND THE OMEGA. I AM THE I AM. I AM THE WAY, THE TRUTH, AND THE LIFE. ANYONE WHO BELIEVES IN ME WILL FIND REST."

I *have not found rest!*

"YOU DO NOT BELIEVE AND TRUST IN ME."

Colsson was brought back to earth when Saul jerked him to his feet. Saul half dragged him to the edge of the clearing and violently threw him down to the ground against the base of a tree. Esau was there with a rope and tied his hands behind the tree.

Colsson didn't even try to resist. He had not the strength, neither the will.

Once Saul and Esau finished their task, they returned to where Timothy was sitting on the ground and Polly was putting together lunch.

While they were eating, Saul said, "You know, Dad, Colsson was pretty serious about resisting a while ago. Are you going to do anything more about it?"

"His actions are one and the same," Timothy growled. "He's starting to think we don't have control over him and that's coming to an end right now."

"Please, Timothy," Polly pleaded. "I don't believe he'll do it again."

"You boys better take her out of here after you help me get set up," said Timothy to Saul and Esau.

"Got it," said Esau with his mouth full.

Polly didn't say anymore, but two small tears formed in her eyes behind her glasses. The sandwich slipped from her hands to the blanket.

Timothy brushed off his hands and stood. He went to his horse and dug around in one of the saddlebags. He took on a confused expression. "Where the blazes is it?" he asked. He felt around more and went around to the other side, checking that saddlebag as well. "Boys, have you seen it?"

Saul and Esau shook their heads. "No," they chorused.

Polly looked up, hope written on her face.

"Don't just sit there, come look for it!" Timothy yelled at the twins.

Saul and Esau jumped to their feet and went to check their saddlebags.

Colsson still sat tied to the tree. He had his chin resting against his chest in an exhausted manner. He was oblivious of the whole thing.

"It's not here, Dad!" called Esau.

"It's not in mine either," reported Saul.

Polly held her breath.

"Maybe I dropped it back there. Mount up and help me look," said Timothy. "Polly, don't you dare touch Colsson!"

Timothy, Saul, and Esau mounted their horses and retreated down the path from which they had come, searching for the lost object.

As soon as the horses were out of sight, Polly slowly rose and crossed the clearing to her horse. She opened the saddlebag and reached inside. Her fingers wrapped around a coil of thick leather. She slowly brought it up, halfway out.

"We must have switched saddlebags," Polly murmured in disbelief. She turned her head back to look at Colsson. His position remained unchanged. She looked back at the whip. Quickly she stuffed it back down deep into the saddlebag and redid the buckles.

When Timothy and the twins returned to the clearing, Timothy was muttering angrily to himself. "I was *sure* I packed it! I don't leave without it. What happened to it? Of all the times it *would* go missing."

God whispered to Colsson, "SEE, EVEN THOUGH YOU DO NOT HAVE FAITH IN ME, I HAVE HELPED YOU FROM THIS TIME. I HAVE HELPED YOU, STUBBORN AS YOU ARE, PRIDEFUL AS YOU ARE, HURT AS YOU ARE. RETURN TO ME."

Colsson looked up. *The whip is gone? But I know it was packed this morning!* His thoughts swirled over the happenings. God had helped him. Could it be Anna was right and he *was* loved?

"What do we do about him now?" asked Esau.

Timothy shook his head. "I do not know, except to leave him as he is until we are ready to go, and make him walk back."

"I guess so," said Saul.

"When do we leave?" asked Polly, almost afraid to ask.

Colsson listened, waiting for Timothy's reply.

"It's about five hours back. I don't want to get back until eleven or twelve o'clock. Which means we have to leave at about six or seven."

"After dinner," said Esau for confirmation.

Timothy nodded. "Yes."

Polly spoke softly after a while of silence. "Timothy."

"What?"

"Hasn't this grudge gone on long enough? Will you ever forgive the Helders?"

90

Timothy clenched his jaw in anger and shook his head. "No! I will never forgive them!"

"Neither will I," Saul declared.

"I won't either," Esau joined in.

"But why?"

"Why have *you* forgiven them?" asked Timothy.

"It was hard for me, but I realized it wasn't their fault. Even if it had been, it's wrong to hold them responsible in such a cruel way." Polly looked over at Colsson, who had gone back to the position he had been holding almost the whole time.

"They killed our son!" Timothy cried hoarsely. "I won't forgive them for that, even if the parents *are* dead."

"That car accident was unavoidable. It wasn't their fault, and it wasn't our son's fault. What if there was family who held a grudge against us for killing Mr. and Mrs. Helder?"

"There isn't," Timothy said firmly.

"I said, *what if*? What if they tried to murder us all for something that was not our fault?"

"I don't want to talk about it anymore," said Timothy.

The sun had begun to set when the Smiths made ready to head back to the main ranch. Once again, Colsson's wrists were tied and the end of the rope tied to the horn of Timothy's saddle.

After they had been traveling for a long time, Colsson's legs finally gave out, and he fell to the ground with a moan. The rope went tight. Splitting pain raced through his shoulders like his arms would be torn from their sockets. He was dragged on his back as Timothy's horse continued.

Timothy's horse felt the extra weight, snorted, tossed his head, and came to a stop right as Colsson released an ear-splitting yell of pain. Timothy cursed.

"Colsson, are you alright?" asked Polly.

"Shut up, Polly," Timothy growled. He twisted in his saddle. "Get up!" he ordered the young man.

Colsson twisted and struggled, groaning helplessly. "I... can't!" With the rope still tight and his hands feeling like they would separate from his wrists, he wasn't getting anywhere in a hurry.

Polly held her breath and dismounted. She sneaked to Saul's horse and felt around in the saddlebag. Her hand wrapped around a small hunting knife. As she approached Colsson, she heard him weeping softly again. She strained her eyes against the dark, searching the ground for the boy. She nearly tripped over him.

Timothy impatiently jerked on the rope, making Colsson cry out again. He cursed. "We might as well just move forward again and *let* him slide on the ground."

"No, Timothy," said Polly. "Give him a chance to get up." She reached Colsson and knelt next to him. "Back up just a little."

"I'm not going to do it," Timothy said defiantly. He clucked to his horse to move forward.

Colsson began to slide again. Tingling pain raced through his arms and shoulders. The rope bit into his flesh. The fabric on his shirt ripped. Worse, he felt blood on his back.

In one smooth motion, Polly drew the hunting knife from its sheath and sliced the rope. Immediately, Polly felt a great burden lifted from her shoulders.

The sudden stop caused Colsson's body to jerk slightly. He grunted softly.

Timothy felt the rope suddenly slack. He pulled it up and felt the end. "Polly!" he cried. He dismounted.

Polly ignored Timothy. She cut the rope from Colsson's hands and helped him to his feet.

Colsson moaned and his legs gave out again. He collapsed to the ground.

Timothy grabbed Polly by the shoulders, spun her around, and shook her violently. "Why did you? I warned you!"

"Timothy, he can't go on foot any longer!"

Timothy shook her again. "Enough!"

"Let him ride from here," Polly pleaded. "We are close to the gate. Aren't we but a few miles from the main part of the ranch? You'd have to let him ride the rest of the distance anyway."

Timothy looked away.

"Timothy, listen to me like you used to," Polly whispered.

Sullenly, Timothy gave in. He jerked Colsson up, dragged him to the spare horse, and tossed him on.

Colsson moaned and swayed, about to fall off the horse. He clutched the horn to stabilize himself. He tried to squeeze the horse's sides with his legs, but he couldn't. His feet hurt like a bed of thorns was thrust through them, and he could barely move them as he struggled to get them into the stirrups. He picked up the reins, but he just couldn't hold on to them. He looped them over the horn. He could barely work his hands after they had been tied for so long. His head sagged without control as they moved along.

As Timothy rode in the lead, he reflected on Polly's words earlier in the day. *"Hasn't this grudge gone on long enough? Will you ever forgive the Helders?"*

What if he did end everything he was doing to Colsson? What if he began to treat Colsson like a son? The accident wasn't Colsson's fault in any way, yet he was suffering for it. For a brief moment, he was glad he had not done any worse to Colsson during the day.

The outside world faded as he reminisced that day. The accident happened close to their house. They'd heard a loud, dramatic crash of steel and glass. Timothy had run all the way to the scene. As he approached, he had stopped in horror. The first thing he saw was a small, dark green car and a man inside. The passenger side was smashed in all the way to the driver's side. The driver's right arm hung out the window, and he was hunched over the steering wheel, eyes closed. Someone pushed him back. His head rolled and sagged until he came to rest against the seat. Blood mingled with his red hair and splotches stood out on his chest. Horrified, Timothy fixed his gaze on the driver's face until a sheet passed over it, obscuring it from view.

"No!" Timothy had cried long and loud in that moment. "Kelly!"

Timothy's horse stumbled slightly. Startled, he gasped and came back to earth. He remembered his pain in losing his oldest son. A tear dripped down his face. His lower lip trembled. Within the next few seconds, the tears multiplied. The quiet sounds grew to a muffled, trembling sob in his throat.

"Kelly is home with Me."

Timothy, in his tears and anguish, remembered why he had adopted Colsson Helder. He thought that by making the Helder's son suffer for Kelly's death, he could leave behind his own pain. He resolved to continue with his original plan. Hate filled him again, and he clutched the horn of his saddle until his hands hurt. His quiet weeping stopped.

Anna awoke with a start when she heard hooves and horses snorting outside. Her heart suddenly quickened when she heard a soft thud on the ground. She threw back the covers and jumped to her feet, running to the open window to look out. She squinted and searched through the thick blackness. As her eyes adjusted, she made out the shapes of horses and the Smiths moving beside them. Wait, where was Colsson? That one was Polly, there was Timothy, and the twins, but what about Colsson?

One of the twins bent over and strained to pull something off the ground. Then he dropped it, bent over again, and frustratingly yanked it. A faint cry reached Anna's ears, and her heart jumped. She recognized Colsson's voice. What had happened? Was that Colsson one of the twins was yanking? Her eyes darted around. Where were the ranch hands? Did they know the Smiths had come back? Was anyone awake and seeing what was going on?

To her relief, Jack ran up to the Smiths. The twin holding Colsson up did so in a more compassionate way when Jack approached.

Anna strained her ears, and sketches of the conversation slowly became clear.

"He's pretty tired, poor guy," Timothy slung a saddlebag over his shoulder. "He's not used to this sort of thing. We're all pretty tired, but I think he feels it the most."

"He looks pretty tired," Jack agreed. "Jake and I will take care of the horses while you all get some rest. Have a good night."

"Thanks," said Timothy.

Jake joined his brother, and they took the horses to the barn.

Anna left the window and returned to her bed. How long before her parents would catch on to what was happening?

In the barn, when the ranch hands were unsaddling the horses, Jake said, "Hey Jack."

"What's up?"

"Come over here a minute."

Jack left the horse he was brushing. "What is it?"

Jake pointed to the horse. "This horse isn't as sweaty as the others. The others are damp all over. This one isn't."

"Why would that be? He's been gone as long as the others."

"That's just it. It's been going as long as the others, but not as hard."

95

Jack spit off to the side. "What should we do now?"

"We should probably tell Mr. Campbell about it. Something doesn't feel right."

"It's probably nothing, Jake, but it seems awful strange. With Mr. Campbell's permission, maybe we should question the Smiths about their activities today."

"Let's try to do that," Jake agreed.

The next day, Jack and Jake talked to Frank while they were standing by the pasture. They told him about the Smiths arriving during the night and finding out one horse wasn't as sweaty as the others were.

"I wouldn't worry about it, fellas," said Frank. "They are granted privacy in business and happenings here. Why the horse wasn't sweaty is for them to know, and us not to worry about."

"Meaning no disrespect, sir, but don't you think it's rather weird?" asked Jake.

"My thought would be one of them wanted to walk a good deal of the way," Frank replied. He slapped the ranch hands' shoulders. "Let's get to work before I have to go in to breakfast."

Colsson was not at the table that morning. After Anna finished serving, she took a plate of breakfast upstairs. She knocked at the door.

"It's locked," she heard Colsson shout. His voice sounded strained, painful, desperate.

Anna unlocked the door and opened it. Colsson was writhing on the floor, holding his arms over his gut. Alarm raced through her. "Colsson, are you okay?"

He couldn't reply. She knelt next to him. With gentle force, she made him turn onto his back. He let out a cry and ripped away, rolling back onto his side.

"Colsson, sit up," Anna commanded, fighting to keep her panic inside. "You're starving." She helped him, then reached for what she had brought.

Immediately he took it and began shoveling it down. While he ate, she asked, "Did you eat anything yesterday?"

He shook his head, keeping his eyes down. His mouth was too full to speak.

Anna sighed and slowly shook her head in despair. How long? How long until this was all over?

When he finished eating, he let out a sigh of relief and leaned his head against the wall.

Anna put her hand on his shoulder. "Are you okay?"

"I'll be alright—" his assurance was cut off. He grunted and squeezed his eyes shut.

"What's wrong?"

"My legs," he groaned. He reached forward to rub them.

As his hand reached forward, Anna saw his wrist, red, the flesh cut, and rope marks firmly imprinted on it. "Colsson!" She took hold of his arm above the marks with one hand, and gently picked up his hand with the other. She slid herself closer to him.

"Please don't," Colsson begged as she examined the marks.

She tore her eyes away from his wrists, concern in her eyes. "What happened?

Colsson wanted to speak immediately, but he held himself back.

"IT'S OKAY. TELL HER."

He heard himself say, "I was tied."

"Why?" Anna's voice shook.

Surprised by the slight quiver in her voice, he looked into her pretty face. He was even more surprised by the heartfelt worry and emotion he saw. Right there, his heart opened to the truth. *I am loved. She does care about me.* His heart softened, and he resolved to let her help him. That was all she wanted. "They tied me so I wouldn't get away, and they made me walk almost the whole time. That's why my legs hurt so much."

"Does it hurt you still?" she lightly brushed the tip of her finger over his wrist.

"Yes." He cringed with pain at Anna's touch. "Can you do anything for it?"

"Come with me," she said gently. "I'll see what I can do."

Colsson forced himself to stand. He grunted, pain shooting through his legs as he took several shaky steps. He followed Anna to the bathroom sink where she ran cool water and guided his wrists under the stream. Finding himself wincing, he clenched his teeth and struggled to keep still. After what seemed like a long time, she shut the water off.

"I'm going to get the aloe. You can go back and sit down if you need." Anna opened a cabinet above the sink.

He left the bathroom. *Did I make the right decision telling her? What if my family sees that she's tended to me? They'll know she's found out about tying me.* A shudder shook his body and soul as he sank to the floor by the window. *If she found out about the—*

Anna broke into his thoughts. She sat cross legged facing him and reached for one of his wrists.

"Anna," he said suddenly, "I don't think you should. If my family finds out you've taken care of me, there's no telling what they'll do. I don't want them to find out that you know what they've been doing."

"I understand," Anna began. She frowned. "But they run the risk of someone seeing your wrists anyway."

"They're going to keep me in here."

Anna rested her elbow on her leg and put her chin in her hand. Her eyebrows lifted. "They're going to lock you in here and let you starve for a week?"

Colsson raised an eyebrow. "You don't believe me, do you?"

Anna's eyes stayed locked in one position, but her head swung in slow half circles.

"They'll keep me alive," he said bitterly.

Anna sighed. "Well at least let me put the aloe on the marks. I won't cover them."

He stretched out his wrists and murmured, "Okay."

"I'm glad you came up, Anna," he said gratefully as she worked. "I've never been helped before."

"Do you want to come to the treehouse today?"

"I don't think I can. I'm too weak and my family is hanging around here all day. Even if they decide to play in the barnyard, I can't just slip away."

Sadly, Anna exhaled. Colsson put his free hand on her shoulder. "I'm sorry, Anna."

"It's okay, Colsson. We can try for another time."

"I want to go, but I can't. That's just the way things are."

A moment of silence passed. Bent over her work, Anna said, "I could tell something was wrong when I saw all of you come into the barnyard late last night."

"They planned a late arrival so nobody would question how exhausted I was. That failed when the two men came for our horses."

"I heard part of the conversation," she admitted. "And I saw one of the twins yanking on you."

He nodded. "That's because I could hardly move."

Anna finished and straightened. "I hope that helps." She went back to the bathroom to replace the aloe.

When she returned, Colsson gazed up at her and gave her a warm smile. "Thank you, Anna."

"Anytime, Colsson," she replied and smiled before she left. She locked the door behind her.

Anna felt terribly disappointed that Colsson couldn't escape. She wanted to be with him so much. He was the only comfort she had since Jack broke off with her. Moreover, Colsson considered her a friend. A close friend, and the only friend he had. For that, she wanted him to always see her as a friend with whom he could hide from his past.

Timothy sat in an easy chair in his room holding a small, framed picture of his son Kelly. He gently fingered the frame, studying Kelly's happy, broadly smiling face. Kelly had red hair and a muscular build like Saul and Esau.

"Kelly," Timothy whispered. His voice catching, he repeated, "Kelly."

Tears dripped down Timothy's face. He sniffled.

Polly came up behind him and laid her hand on his shoulder.

He briefly took his eyes away from the treasured picture to look up at Polly, then his eyes returned to Kelly's face.

"I miss him," Timothy whispered.

Polly nodded. "I do too."

"Why was he taken away from us? Why did he have to get into the accident?"

Polly squeezed Timothy's shoulder. "I don't know, and I don't expect to ever find out."

Timothy laid the picture on his lap and looked off into space, reminiscing. His hand reached up to hold Polly's hand. "We were such a happy family before this happened. And Kelly—" he broke off. "When Kelly came home from work, we'd all light up. He'd walk in the door, and anything annoying or angering that had happened at my work, I forgot. Completely. I loved Kelly."

"We all loved Kelly," she murmured.

"It is a horrible thing to have love torn from you like that."

"We still love him. We don't stop loving someone, even when they are gone. It's just, there's an unhealable ache in our hearts because we *do* love him."

"Not even going somewhere on vacation can erase it," he agreed. "Like coming here. This has done nothing."

"We needed to get out of the house for a while. Coming here was never a bad thing."

"I know." He picked up Kelly's picture again. "Whenever I see his face, I just wish someone understood."

"Well, what about Colsson?" she asked sharply. "He suffered a loss. The loss of his parents."

"He doesn't even remember. He doesn't even know we're not his real parents."

Polly bit her lip.

"I wish I were like Colsson and could forget it all. I wish I could forget about losing Kelly." Timothy squeezed his eyes closed, struggling to hold the tears back.

Polly gave his hand a gentle squeeze. "On the other hand, I always want to remember Kelly, remember back to when he was still with us and how happy we all were. I want his memory to live with us forever."

Chapter Eight

Whenever Colsson was able to safely leave his room, he accompanied Anna to her special place. There, he was no longer a shy boy cowering from every shadow or movement. He was a man. In a quiet, invisible way, Anna seemed to strengthen him to become a real man. He left his past behind whenever he was with her.

Colsson felt strength and courage flow into him more every day. Independence and longing to be free from his tyrant father's clutches and with Anna weighed on him. He searched for a way to become a man of his own. Defiance of cowering to Timothy mounted to great heights inside him. Day by day, he waited for his chance...

And then, it came. One morning, Timothy entered the boys' room. Colsson looked up and searched his face as he spoke to Saul and Esau. Fear spread to the farthest reaches of his body. That look was back. The look of anguish in Timothy's eyes that he never understood. The look that came before the times he especially suffered. All the strength and courage he thought he had vanished within that second. Hope faded. Dreams were lost. Fear took hold.

Colsson clutched the horn of his saddle, his knuckles a brilliant white. His jaw he clenched tight until his muscles hurt. The whole family was going back to the clearing they had been to before.

As before, Timothy dismounted and opened the gate. When

he remounted, his voice rang sharply and clearly, filling Colsson with pure dread. "Off, Colsson."

Colsson's foot slid back out of the stirrup, and he rose slightly out of the safety of the saddle. Leather creaked and metal clinked. He stopped midway and cast his gaze down to his hand. He still held the reins in his hand as he clutched the horn. He released his hold on the horn slightly. The reins lay calmly and quietly in his snow white palm. "What am I doing?" he murmured to himself. Courage and determination came back, and he made up his mind to take this one chance.

Firmly, he sat back in the saddle and took a determined hold on the reins. Without a word to his family, who never noticed his hesitation, he gave their backs a steely glare. He wheeled his horse sharply and jabbed his heels against the horse's sides. The horse immediately responded, galloping.

Alerted by the noise, the Smiths turned in their saddles. Timothy didn't waste any time. "Let's go!"

Timothy, Saul, and Esau rode after Colsson.

Colsson turned toward the east.

The chase was on!

Hope filled Colsson. A brief smile came across his face as he panted. He knew he was the better rider. He turned around to look behind him. Saul and Esau slipped and slid from side to side in their saddles. He chuckled. It was all they could do to hang on. A thrill shot through him. Like a prisoner with his chains broken, his spirits soared as he raced through a prairie. The horse rocked beneath him, loving the run. He looked straight ahead, lifted his voice, and whistled sharply to the horse.

Colsson looked behind him again. Timothy was gaining. He looked ahead and aimed his horse north, toward the timbered hills. Once in the forest, he slowed his horse to navigate through the timber. Looking behind, he felt sure Timothy couldn't see him, and turned his horse west, in the direction of the gate. He circled south and exited the thicket behind Timothy and aimed directly for the main ranch. The horse loped easily in the direction of his commands.

Thundering hooves caught the attention of several people. Colsson galloped into the barnyard. He dismounted near the barn and began removing the tack. Anna hurried up to him. The guests, thinking nothing of his arrival, returned to their activities.

"Colsson, what happened? How did you manage to get back?"

"I knew how to ride," he replied, dragging the saddle off the horse's back. "They didn't know I can ride. So, when they told me to get off, I simply rode away." He fluttered his hand toward the distance for effect.

Anna laughed, relieved. She threw her arms around his neck, hugging him tightly. Together, they put away the saddle, saddle blanket, and the bridle, then brushed the horse down and worked the sweat out of his coat.

"Colsson, what will they do when they get ahold of you?" Anna looked across the horse's back, worried.

Colsson shrugged and shook his head. "I don't know, but I'm not really afraid of them anymore. The worst they can do now is they'll try to starve me. But that's not a big deal because that's taken care of." He looked Anna in the eye. "And if they try to take me somewhere, they know I'll just ride away again. I can't think of much else."

"What about when you have to leave?" she managed to say.

He sighed and looked down. "I'll have to go back with them. There's no way I can escape them then."

Later that day, Colsson sat in his room, anticipating for the return of his family. When the door finally opened, Timothy marched in, followed by the twins.

Timothy's face was red, his eyes narrow slits, and his jaw tight with his teeth ground together. He stood with clenched fists.

"*You!*" Timothy jabbed his finger at Colsson.

A frightened tingle shot through Colsson's spine.

"Why did you do it? You know what happens when you attempt such things."

"I do, and I don't fear it."

Saul pushed in front of Timothy. "Why not?" he demanded.

"Because I know you're not going to pull anything here. If you try to take me back there, I'll just leave again. You can't lead my horse, because people will see you and want to know why it is you start leading my horse. And if you try to lead my horse when we are out of sight, I will leave before you try."

Timothy couldn't say anything more. Colsson knew he was hacked to the bone. Timothy spun and left, slamming the door behind him.

As time went on, when Anna and Colsson spent time together, her heart grew heavier and heavier knowing the time when the Smiths would go home would be soon. She dreaded having to ask her parents about it, but not knowing was making her nervous.

Finally, one evening, Anna got up the nerve to ask. "Mom, do you know when the Smiths are leaving?"

Liesel was at the desk in the lobby. It was after dinner, and Anna was aching to know even though she was scared to find out.

Liesel flipped through the guest book. "In a couple days," she replied.

Numbness swept through Anna. "A couple days?" she

repeated hoarsely. She rested the heel of her hands on the desk and supported herself as she stared unblinkingly at the desktop.

Liesel looked up at Anna. "Anna, what's wrong with you?"

"Time has flown," she murmured. She weakly left the desk, went to her room, and to lay on her bed. "God, what can I do? How can I keep Colsson from going back with them?"

Over and over, she echoed the prayer in her mind. After a few minutes, she said aloud, "He's got to get away. That's the only thing."

The next day when the Smiths were at lunch and Anna noticed Colsson wasn't there, she hurried up to his room with a couple sandwiches and knocked at the room door.

"Come in," Colsson called.

Anna went in. "Colsson, you've got to get away!" she blurted as soon as she closed the door. "Your family is leaving in a couple days, and you just can't go with them."

He shook his head. "It's not any use, Anna. If they found out and caught me—" he broke off and hastily turned his head to the window.

Anna crossed the room. "Go on horseback. It's the easiest way. And if I act as if I don't know about anything, like you're still at the ranch, they may play along and leave to avoid suspicion. They would make it look like you're with them when they leave." She knelt next to him. "You've got to get away."

He kept his gaze down at the barnyard. "I just can't. The risk is more than I can bear."

"But what if you manage to get away until I can make my parents understand?" she pressed.

He shrugged and looked at her. "I don't have anywhere to go."

"Here," she said. "Wait for a little while, then come back here."

He turned back to the window. Anna held his shoulders and turned him to look her in the eye. "What's the risk if you don't get away?"

He said nothing, but he contemplated on what Anna said for a long time. Finally, he nodded. "Deep down, I...I know you're right. I'd better get away while I can."

He stood and tucked a couple changes of clothes into his small case. Anna ran downstairs and, since Liesel wasn't there, she put together as much food as she could for him.

As Anna watched him skillfully saddle Butterscotch, she had a strange feeling, something she had never felt before. She didn't want him to go. How long until he would be back? Would he come back? What would become of him? Would his family find him? Would something terrible happen if they did? Would she ever see him again?

Colsson wrestled with his own feelings inside. He didn't want to leave as much as Anna didn't want him to leave. Now that he cared about Anna the way he did, he never wanted to be away from her ever again.

Butterscotch stamped an impatient foot. He blew through his nostrils and shook his mane back and forth.

"All right, we'll be going in a minute," he assured the horse. He turned to Anna. "I'll be on my way," he whispered.

Anna nodded. She felt a lump in her throat preventing her from answering.

He tried to find words to talk to her. "Anna, I..." he stopped and took a deep breath. "I want to..." he gave up searching for words and instead pulled Anna close to his chest. He held her tightly.

Anna blinked back tears and wrapped her arms around his stick-thin form. Despite her efforts to keep them in, two tears rolled down her cheeks.

He let her go and gently pushed her hair behind her ear. "I want you to know how much I appreciate all you have done for me, Anna," he said. He squeezed her hand and swung up on Butterscotch. He gave her a smile and kicked Butterscotch into a canter, unable to say anything more.

Though Anna was sorry to see him leave, she was glad he was getting away and escaping his horrible life.

The next morning, Liesel came in the kitchen upset. Anna looked up from her work, but before she had a chance to ask what was wrong, Liesel told her, "Colsson has disappeared. The Smiths can't find him anywhere." Liesel narrowed her eyes, put her hands on her hips, and looked right at Anna. "And I think you know what happened."

Anna's heart skipped a beat. "Yes, Mom, I...I do. I encouraged him to leave."

"Why?" Liesel demanded.

Anna took a deep breath. "He isn't being treated justly. I don't know everything that's happened to him, but one thing I know for sure is they starve him. That's why he's so skinny."

The anger in Liesel's voice turned to alarm. "They *what*?" she shrieked. "Anna, how did you find out?"

Keeping her eyes on her work, Anna replied, "Colsson told me."

"I never thought the Smiths would deliberately starve him! Why didn't you tell us?"

"I tried, but you and Dad didn't listen or believe me."

Liesel went to the door leading to the dining room and looked through a crack at the Smith family, who were just sitting down at the table. How could it be? The Smiths were such friendly people! They wouldn't ever starve their own son. Would they? Liesel turned back to see her daughter, who was watching her. She realized right then that she needed to trust Anna.

"If you're right, Anna, and they are starving Colsson, we need to talk to your father immediately."

"Talk to me about what?" asked Frank as he came in the kitchen.

Liesel exhaled and looked her husband in the eye.

Anna's heart beat wildly as she prayed for God's will on the matter. Whatever it may be.

"The Smiths have been starving Colsson, Frank."

Frank furrowed his eyebrows. "How do you know?"

Liesel cast a deliberate glance at Anna. "Anna told me just now. Colsson told her. What's more, it makes sense as he's not always at the table."

Frank looked through the crack. "Where is he now?"

Anna stammered, "I encouraged him to leave. He left yesterday."

Surprisingly calm and without looking away from the crack, Frank said, "I'm glad of that." He left his post. "Question is, what do we do now?"

"What do you mean?" asked Liesel. "If they are mistreating Colsson, don't we have to tell the authorities?"

"We can't prove anything. We ourselves don't know for sure."

"But hadn't we at least tell them?" asked Liesel.

"Yes, I'm going to tell them about our suspicions. And the sooner the better. I'll be back in a minute. I don't want anyone to overhear me."

Frank left to call the sheriff's office from his room. A minute later, as Anna was serving at the Smiths' table, one of the guests asked the Smiths, "Where is your other boy?"

Timothy replied, "He wasn't feeling well enough to come down so he's still resting."

"What a shame," said another guest.

The first guest asked, "Is he sick?"

Esau replied, "He has a weak digestive system, and it causes him to feel sickly a lot of the time."

Anna returned to the kitchen. What a startling discovery about the Smiths! How could they lie so effortlessly?

"The Smiths just lied about Colsson," Anna said flatly.

"Something is going on, and they cannot get away with it," Frank said firmly. He sighed. "Anna, I am truly sorry for not listening to you when you first thought something was wrong with Colsson. I know you always tell the truth, but I didn't even think it possible for anything to be wrong. The Smiths seemed like such a wonderful family, but I think they pulled the wool over my eyes. Some people are capable of lying and having no conscience. I don't know what or why they are doing this, but a deputy is on his way over. It'll take him about an hour or so to get here."

When the deputy arrived, Frank was waiting for him in front of the ranch house. Frank explained the situation to him and led him inside to the Timothy and Polly's bedroom.

The deputy knocked, and Timothy opened the door. The deputy showed Timothy his badge and ID card. "Deputy Sanders of the Meadowbrook Sheriff's Department. Mr. Campbell called me because of your son."

"Yes, sir," said Timothy. "Would you come in please?"

Contrary to what Frank expected, Timothy seemed relieved to see the deputy and not at all alarmed.

"My son disappeared sometime yesterday afternoon. I don't know why, but we think it strange as we were planning on leaving tomorrow." Timothy sank into the recliner.

"Do you have any idea as to why he might have gone?" asked Deputy Sanders.

Timothy shook his head, and Polly added in, "It doesn't make any sense to us. We never imagined he'd even think of leaving."

"What's his name?"

"Colsson."

"What is his age?"

"Nineteen."

"Do you know where he might have gone?"

"No," said Timothy.

"I need a picture of him if you have one."

"We don't have a picture, unfortunately," said Polly.

"Could he possibly have run away because he didn't want to leave here?"

"He was always so submissive," Polly said. "Even if he wanted to stay, he wouldn't have said anything."

"How would you describe him?"

Timothy and Polly looked at each other. "He's fairly tall," Polly started.

"Blond hair, lean, blue-green eyes, and he's fairly quiet," Timothy continued.

Deputy Sanders made more notes. "Is there anyone else in your family I might talk to?"

Timothy rose from his chair and rapped on the wall. He sat back down, and the twins came in. As soon as they saw the deputy, their eyes narrowed.

"What does he want with us?" Saul asked. He cursed under his breath. Esau crossed his arms and swore in a low, unheard voice.

"Boys! Boys!" shouted Timothy. "He's here to help look for your brother."

"Do you know where your brother might have gone or why he left?" asked Deputy Sanders.

"All I know is he made a lot of trouble for us," Esau growled.

"How would we know as to where he might have gone?" Saul added.

"Excuse me, deputy," said Polly. "But can we have a guarantee of privacy from the other guests?"

Deputy Sanders raised an eyebrow. "I cannot guarantee privacy ma'am. I may have to question the boarders with Mr. Campbell's permission," he finished with a glance and nod at Frank.

"If you find that you need to, sir, I am happy to oblige," Frank replied readily.

Deputy Sanders asked Esau and Saul a couple more question then closed his notebook. "I'd best get started looking. Mr. Campbell, could I possibly talk to your wife and daughter before starting a search?"

"Yes, sir," Frank replied.

He and Deputy Sanders left the room.

Anna told Deputy Sanders everything she knew and had found, including the bloody sheets under the bed almost a month ago. She repeated what Colsson said about the sheets, about being starved, and multiple other things she thought as strange.

"And you encouraged him to leave because of what he told you?" asked the deputy.

Anna nodded. "Yes, sir. I don't know everything that is going on, but I did encourage him to leave because of what little he told me."

"Is there anyone who might verify that he left yesterday afternoon and on horseback?"

"There were a few guests playing volleyball when he left," Anna admitted. "I don't know if they saw him leave or not, though."

Deputy Sanders closed his notebook. "May I speak to some of the guests?"

Frank led the deputy outside to where the volleyball queen, Terra, had already started a game with some of the others. Deputy Sanders confirmed Colsson's description and the fact he had left the day before. When he had finished and was walking with Frank back to his car, he looked over some of his notes.

"I'll get started on this case right away," he said. "I'm going to start at the Smiths' house to find out what I can about possible activities."

Frank shook the deputy's hand. "Thank you for your time, sir."

"It's my duty," Deputy Sanders replied. "And I am glad to be of service to those who need me."

Chapter Nine

Colsson rode into the barnyard at sunset three days later. He dismounted Butterscotch.

Jack came up to him. "Glad to see you're back."

"Hello," said Colsson, unsure of what to say.

Jack took Butterscotch's reins. "I'll take care of him."

Colsson smiled. At last, he would be able to eat without anyone holding him back. He would have enough. "Thanks." He turned and hurried toward the ranch house, a welcome sight.

"Wait, Colsson!" Jack cried.

Colsson slowed down briefly, turning back slightly to see the ranch hand. "Dinner's going to be soon!"

Jack waved a desperate hand. "No, don't!"

He shook his head, grinning. "I'm going to be late!"

"Wait, I need to tell you something!"

"Tell me later, huh?" Too happy to care about anything, he disregarded Jack's cries. He jogged a few steps before returning to a fast walk.

A curtain on the third floor moved slightly, and a set of eyes peered down right at him. Little did he know the plan had failed, and the Smiths had stayed behind to look for him.

Stopping long enough to wash the dirt and sweat off his face and hands, Colsson eagerly made his way to the dining room and opened the door quickly. The smile on his face disappeared. The Smiths were still at the ranch! Fear flooded into his eyes, and his heart rate quickened. If only he'd listened to Jack.

All eyes in the dining room turned to see Colsson. An uncomfortable, stony silence fell on the room.

"Well don't just stand there," said Timothy. "Sit down."

Scarcely daring to breath, Colsson sat in his usual place. Timothy leaned over and murmured, "You're going to wish you *hadn't* pulled that stunt. You are going to regret it."

"When did you get back?" asked someone from the other side of the room.

Colsson kept his eyes on his plate and his hands in his lap. "Just now."

Anna stood next to him while serving. With her free hand, she squeezed his shoulder, wishing she could tell him she was sorry, and she would have told him to stay away if she had a chance.

Colsson, who had been so happy to be back, now felt defeated. His shoulders slumped in despair, but he gave Anna a tiny smile.

The Smiths told Colsson over and over how worried they had been and how happy they were to have him back. They scolded him for leaving and for worrying them.

Anna couldn't believe how well they were faking their feelings. They couldn't fool her.

"Colsson is back," Anna told her parents when she returned to the kitchen.

"He is?" said Liesel. She creased her brow in worry. "Frank, what do we do now?"

"There is only so much we *can* do," Frank replied. "I'll call Deputy Sanders right away. Let's give Colsson a different room in a different location."

After dinner, Anna, Frank, and Liesel sought a chance to talk to Colsson in private, but at least one of the Smiths was always standing close beside him. After trying for an hour in vain, Anna went to her room frustrated and worried. What could she do? "God, please help me," she begged. "Please help me. Please help me."

"HIS ROOM," a voice whispered in her mind.

Immediately Anna leapt from her bed and darted upstairs to the boys' room. She knocked but received no answer. She felt for her keys. Hesitation tingled in her spine and fingertips as she reached for the knob. Expelling her breath, she gripped it and opened the door, closing it behind her. "Colsson?" she called. She looked all around the room, but he wasn't there.

A noise from outside the room made her heart jump. The next instant, the door opened, and someone shoved Colsson inside the room. He fell to the floor with a loud grunt. The door was slammed shut and locked it from the outside.

Colsson hastily got up and tried to open the door, but failed.

"Colsson," Anna whispered.

Startled, he spun around. Fear was written over his face. He relaxed slightly when he saw her, but the fear in his eyes remained. "Anna," he whispered in relief.

She ran to him and hugged him tightly. "I'm sorry," she whispered. "I would have told you they were still here, but I couldn't."

A lonely tear dripped down Colsson's cheek. He squeezed his eyes shut to prevent more. "It's okay," he choked quietly as he let her go.

"Why did you come back so soon?"

He slowly shook his head. "I didn't feel safe, as I should have. I didn't want to be anywhere but here." He looked at her in the eyes. "Now that I have a true friend, I couldn't bear to be gone." He gave her a wry smile before dropping his head. "Besides, my food supply didn't hold out."

Anna managed a tiny smile and a weak chuckle. She rubbed his shoulder. "My dad said to give you a different room. We've been trying to talk to you ever since dinner was over, but we couldn't. I'll show you your room now."

Colsson looked to the door, then said, "Anna, we can't."

"Why?"

He looked back at her. "We're locked in."

"We can just unlock it."

"I've never been able to."

A chill shot down Anna's spine. She sat on the floor in complete shock. "They jimmied it!"

"Who did *what?*"

"Your family jimmied the lock. It's supposed to lock *and* unlock from the inside and outside. They messed with the lock so it couldn't be unlocked from in here. It never occurred to me before."

"What do we do?" he asked. "I've never really cared or thought about getting out before, but this is different. *You're* in here."

She struggled to keep her throat from tightening. Only someone outside the door could unlock it. It might be hours before her parents found them, and the Smiths might find her there first.

"God, what should I do?" she prayed aloud. "I can't do this alone. Show me the way."

The cold look Colsson got whenever he heard the name of the Lord returned. "Why bother to pray?" he demanded. "How can you—"

She stood and grabbed him by the shoulders. "Believe, Colsson. Have faith He will hear you and help you in His good time. Before I came up here, I prayed for help, and He led me up here."

"If He listened to you, why won't He listen to someone going through the worst life imaginable?" he asked, his voice hardening.

"He helps in His good time," Anna said softly. "But He asks that you have faith and believe in Him. He asks that you listen to His voice. And those who suffer for a good cause on earth are rewarded in heaven, and those who spend their time doing evil, though they may seem well off and happy, they will spend eternity in hell."

She crossed the room, looking for a way out.

He stood in his place. "Hell?" he repeated. "I've heard of it before, but what is it, really?"

Trying to find a way to get out of the room left Anna's mind instantly. She sat on the floor and indicated to him to do the same. "Hell," she began, "is a place of suffering no one can even imagine. The Bible describes it as a lake of fire and brimstone, a place where those who are evil are thrown. They stay there forever and ever, and they never die. They are burning up, and the pain is only known by them that are in it."

"I'd rather go there than be unhappy and hurting on earth," he said bitterly.

"Colsson, you don't understand. Hell is the most wretched place. Here on earth you don't live forever. There will come a time when you will die and leave the earth behind. You have a choice. You can suffer and burn forever, or you may live in joy and peace forever. Which would you choose?"

"It doesn't work that way, Anna. Even I know that."

"It is real, and you will face it one day," Anna said firmly. "Even if you want to live in happiness forever, if you do not rely on the Lord and live as He wants you to, you are rebelling against the Lord, and you will be punished. I don't want to see you go there."

He looked up sharply. "Are you telling me that's where I'm going?"

"I believe you are, if you continue to rebel against the Lord as you are now."

"I don't care."

"You will, once you come to face your Maker." Anna stood. "Please think about what I have said, Colsson."

He bit his lip. Anna paced the room, again attempting to find a way out. The window caught her eye, and she opened it. The sun was setting, but it was still light outside.

"Colsson, we can climb down the ivy," she said.

He stood next to her as she continued, "There's a long ladder running down alongside the windows, but the ivy has almost hidden it. It's still usable."

"I think I remember that mentioned," he said. "Your mom told us about that when we first came. It's there in case of a fire, right?"

"Right." She climbed out the window and cautiously climbed down the ladder.

Colsson followed her.

As they climbed carefully down, he said, "I wish I had remembered about this. I could have escaped many times."

Once they reached the ground, Anna led the way to the back door and took him inside to the kitchen.

"Where were you?" asked Liesel.

"Locked in Colsson's room," said Anna. "I was up there when someone pushed Colsson in and locked the door from the outside."

"Saul," Colsson cut in.

"The door's lock was jimmied so no one can unlock it from the inside. We got out through the window. Where's Dad?"

"I don't know," said Liesel. "He went to look for you. He might be out in the barn."

Frank's voice came from behind them. "I saw you two come down the ladder."

"Yes. Saul locked Colsson in the room," Anna explained. "The lock has been jimmied."

"What should we do now?" asked Liesel.

"Deputy Sanders can't come out here tonight," said Frank. "But he's going to come out first thing in the morning."

"Where do we put him for tonight?"

Frank thought for a minute. "Probably close to our room. As close as we can get him."

While the Campbells were talking, a crouched figure in the laundry room listened behind the closed door. After Frank made his decision, the figure retreated away to the room at the end of the hall on the third floor.

"Anna, will you take Colsson to the room right next to ours?"

"Of course, Dad."

She led Colsson to the room to the left of Frank and Liesel's. She unlocked the door and let him in. The room looked identical to the one he shared with his brothers with a window straight across from the door and the bed to the left against the wall.

"This is all mine?" he asked.

"Yes."

"I've never had a room of my own before," he said as though entranced. He wandered to the neatly made bed. He turned back to Anna. "May I sit on it?"

Anna wanted to say, "You goose, it's for you, why ask?" but instead she solemnly said, "Of course, Colsson."

He eased himself down slowly onto the bed. "It's so soft!" he whispered in delight. He ran his hand over the quilt.

"Lie back," Anna instructed. She gently pushed his shoulders back. But as soon as his back touched the bed, he squeezed his eyes shut and cried out. He quickly forced his back up and rolled onto his side.

Anna's hand flew to her mouth. "Colsson, did I hurt you?"

He shook his head. "No, it's okay."

"Does your back hurt you?"

He gritted his teeth and nodded. "It's okay, though."

"Do you usually sleep on your side?"

"Yes. Is this where I sleep?"

"Unless you prefer to sleep on the floor," Anna said carelessly as she took the pillow from under the covers.

"No!" he suddenly shouted. He supported himself with his arms, and a scared look crossed his face. "Please let me stay here!"

"Colsson, did you think I wouldn't?" she asked gently. "What are you afraid of?"

He didn't answer, but he stared at her for a long time, breathing heavily.

She put her hand on his shoulder and looked him in the eye. "You don't have to be afraid," she said softly. "I promise." She guided him down so his head was resting on the pillow.

Little by little, he slowly relaxed. He didn't move for a long time. "I've never slept in a bed," he whispered.

"What do you mean? Is that why I saw you on the floor about a month ago instead of on the bed?"

He closed his eyes and nodded. "I've slept on the floor for as long as I can remember."

"Is that something else your family does to you?"

He nodded again.

She brushed a strand of his blond hair off his forehead. "I'm sorry," she whispered.

ANNE KRISTALIN SPANFELNER

He didn't answer. His side rose and fell evenly, and his eyes remained closed. Anna stood and went to the door. She turned and looked back at the sleeping boy, then closed the door behind her.

Anna returned to the kitchen. "I just found out Colsson hasn't ever slept in a bed."

"What do you mean he hasn't ever slept in a bed before?" asked Frank.

"The Smiths make him sleep on the floor."

"So that's why you found sheets under the bed," said Liesel. "They were spread out on the floor for him."

Anna frowned. "I sort of forgot about that."

"Shouldn't we have Jack and Jake take turns guarding Colsson?" Liesel asked Frank.

Frank chewed his lip. "I think he'll be safe for tonight. As long as the Smiths don't know where he is, they can't get to him. Plus, you and I sleep nearby. They won't try any funny stuff."

"But won't they find out he's gone from the boys' room and try to find him?"

"If they do, we tell them nothing. This is one time when it's better to lie."

"But what do we tell them?"

"We don't know where he is," Frank replied simply.

Saul rapped on Timothy and Polly's door. Timothy opened the door. "Well?" he demanded. "Where is he? How did he escape?"

Saul stepped inside the room and closed the door behind himself. "I have no idea how he got out except someone must have seen us and let him out. The Campbells are planning to put him in the room right next to theirs."

123

"Do you know where that is?"

"Yeah, if you stand facing the ranch house in the barnyard, the second window from the left on the first floor is theirs. The one all the way to the left is their daughter's. So the third window..."

"Right," said Timothy as Saul trailed off. "About one o'clock tonight, we're going to get him and beat it out of here."

"Not back home?"

"No." Timothy paced the floor. "One thing we know for sure is the Campbells are on to us now. We can't go back home."

"Ah," said Saul knowingly. He grinned. "I think I know where we might be going."

Timothy pointed to Saul. "Exactly. That's where we're headed. We'll hide there for a while."

"Got it," said Saul. "I'll tell Esau, and we'll get ready."

"Get on it," Timothy ordered.

Chapter Ten

"Why aren't the Smiths down here yet?" Anna asked her mother when she returned from getting dirty breakfast dishes from the dining room.

Liesel looked up from loading the dishwasher. "They haven't come down yet?"

"No, they haven't. I haven't seen Colsson either."

Liesel looked at the clock. "It's nine o'clock, and breakfast is over."

Frank put down the newspaper he was reading at the table. "We better find out what's going on. Anna, you go check in on Colsson. I'll check in on the Smiths upstairs."

Anna immediately left and went to Colsson's room. She knocked at his door. There was no answer. She knocked again. No answer. *He must be sleeping still, poor guy.*

Frank came down a minute later. "The Smiths are gone," he announced.

"Gone?" Liesel cried. "What do you mean?"

"They're gone. They've left the ranch. They must have packed up and left early this morning. The only explanation for how they got away is they went out the window."

Anna didn't wait to hear more. She raced back to Colsson's room. As she opened the door, she breathed a silent prayer that Colsson wasn't gone.

Her fears were true. Colsson was gone. Except for the bed slightly mussed, the room looked undisturbed. Did the Smiths take him with them? They must have! But how did they know where Colsson was? She crossed the room to the window. It was open just a crack as though someone hadn't closed it all the way.

She hurried back to the kitchen, on the verge of tears. Frank had just hung up on the phone. "Deputy Sanders is on his way over," he said. "Is Colsson gone?"

Anna nodded and took a deep breath, struggling to control her emotions. "He must have gone out through the window. It was open slightly."

Frank and Liesel looked at each other.

Anna took another deep breath. "I—I think I need some time alone. I'm going to go to the treehouse."

Liesel hugged her and murmured, "We'll get him back."

She blinked hard and nodded, wishing she could speak. She left the house and rode Emerald to her special place. She felt afraid for Colsson's sake. What would happen to him?

When the deputy arrived, he searched Colsson's room. "Window's been forced," he announced. "I need to check out the third-floor rooms."

The Smiths' rooms were clean. They'd left the house through the windows and left nothing behind. They hadn't even slept in their beds.

"They could be miles away by now," Deputy Sanders said grimly. "It doesn't make sense for them to go back to their house, but we'll check there anyway."

"Why wouldn't it make sense for them to go back to their house?" Liesel inquired.

"I obtained a search warrant and searched their house for their son. I found certain evidence against them," explained Deputy Sanders. "Abuse has been confirmed."

Liesel's heart skipped a beat, and Frank felt a chill go down his spine.

"What kind of abuse?" asked Liesel.

"I'm not permitted to reveal that," said Deputy Sanders. "If you are willing, may I speak to your other guests?"

"Of course," said Frank. He and Liesel led the deputy downstairs again.

Never before had Anna realized how much she cared about Colsson. He'd come to be a very dear friend to her, and she wanted to help him in every way she could. What could she do now that he was gone? What would happen to him? She sat on the floor in her treehouse and buried her head in her arms, trying to hold back the tears slipping through her eyes and running down her cheeks.

"God, why did you take him away?" she sobbed. "You know all that is happening to him, and how much he needs You to help him. Please be with him. Please help Deputy Sanders find him before—" She broke off as the tears began afresh.

Anna stayed where she was for a long time. She struggled to push away horrible thoughts of Colsson starving to death.

When finally Anna came down from the treehouse, she mounted Emerald, but instead of heading for home, she unintentionally walked her horse through the meadow beyond the brook. Too distressed to realize what she was doing, she gave the mare her head like she always did when she was returning home from her special place.

Emerald walked through an open gate at the edge of the ranch, guided by an unseen Hand. Anna, lost in her thoughts, didn't notice when they reached new territory that was not a part of the ranch. Emerald continued walking with her preoccupied rider until she was miles into the back country.

A tree branch slapped Anna in the face. Startled, she came to her senses with a yelp. She stopped Emerald and looked all around. "Oh, no," she groaned. "How could I be so stupid? We've left the ranch! I've never been out here before."

Anna dismounted. They were in the heavily timbered hills that began just past the meadow and stretched on to the edge of the ranch and beyond as far as the eye could see.

"What am I going to do? I have to find my way back to the ranch, but which way is it?"

Emerald snorted impatiently. Anna remounted. "I don't have a choice but to give you your head," she said to her mare.

Emerald continued walking but directed her course a little to the left. After a few minutes, they came to a small clearing. "This isn't right," Anna said to herself. "I think I need to go back the way we came."

Instead of readily responding to Anna's command to turn, Emerald stood still. Her ears pricked curiously, then flattened.

"Emerald, what is wrong with you?" Anna asked. "It's getting late, and I've got to get back!" She tried again to turn Emerald, but the mare resisted, snorting and tossing her head.

Anna slapped the mare's rump and called to her to turn. Emerald shied away and snorted again. Anna dismounted. What was wrong with her horse?

"Come on, Emerald," she said angrily, yanking at the lead rein tied to the sides of the halter. Emerald balked and refused to move. The mare held her ears back and pawed the ground.

Anna sat down on the ground, frustrated. "God, help me," she begged.

Emerald put her nose to the ground, jerked her head up, and snorted. Anna creased her forehead. "What is it, girl?" She crawled on her hands and knees to the place Emerald had just put her nose.

Her eyes widened in terror. The grass was stained red. She pulled a small handful. A small scrap of cloth lay nearby, also stained red. She picked it up. "Colsson!" she whispered. Her mind flashed back to the sheets she found under the bed day after the Smiths had arrived.

Her mother's words echoed in her mind. *"He has a condition that causes him to bleed easily."* Something more was going on. The Smiths were doing more to Colsson than starving him. Blood? How did that fit into the picture?

Anna looked at the grass in her hand. A chill swept through her body. Whatever was happening, she knew she needed to go back and tell her parents and Deputy Sanders. She mounted Emerald and prayed the mare would go this time. She nudged Emerald behind her ribs. "Let's go, Emerald," she said firmly, struggling to conceal the fear in her voice from herself.

Emerald started immediately. Anna gave the mare her head, hoping her horse knew the way to the ranch. She knew at least a couple miles lay between her and the ranch border.

Emerald went on for hours. To Anna, they seemed to be going deeper into the heart of the hills. But, at last, she heard the rushing of the brook. Relief surged through her. She could follow it downstream to the ranch. Once she found the ranch, she could ride straight back to the house.

After Anna and Emerald drank from the brook, Anna mounted Emerald again and they continued on. They hadn't gone far when a scream tore through the quiet stillness of the forest. Emerald stopped and tossed her head.

Anna's heart flew to her throat as she nervously looked all around her. Mountain lions could be found around these woods, and they screamed like a woman. But somehow, the scream she heard sounded different. It hadn't sounded quite like the mountain lions she'd heard before when they came near the main ranch.

Still watching with all senses alert, she nudged Emerald to a walk.

A minute later, there was a sudden snap and another cry. Anna gave a tiny shriek and cranked her head to stare at the branches. Was that a branch cracking she had heard before the second scream? Another snap sounded, and Emerald began nervously tossing her head and prancing. A minute later, they broke through the forest into a clearing much larger than the one they'd left behind hours ago. But what surprised Anna the most was a log shack in the middle of the shadowy clearing. Moss grew on the roof, and the logs were weathered and gray. "A miner's shack?" Anna asked herself. She stopped Emerald.

Suddenly, there was another snap, followed by a low, long cry. Immediately after it died down, someone yelled at the top of their lungs, "What did you tell them?"

Anna turned white and she froze to her horse. She knew that voice. *Timothy!* "No!" she whispered hoarsely.

She kicked Emerald to a canter toward the shack, abandoning her own safety. She circled the shack to reach the door on the other side. She flew off Emerald before the mare came to a full stop and ran inside.

The shack was empty! The floor shook beneath her. A trapdoor in the corner of the room caught her eye. She rushed to it, lifted it, and went down the wood steps. At the bottom of the stairs was a room made out of stone and clay that was at least double the size of the shack. One small window at the level of the ground let just enough light in to see. While Anna's eyes adjusted to the dim light, something heavy fell against her, knocking her to the floor. Warm liquid ran down her body.

Shapes began to form. She recognized one of the twins standing across the room from her, another twin standing to the left side of the room, Polly standing on the right, and Timothy standing in the middle. Anna's heart beat wildly inside her chest. She was reliving her nightmare.

"What the—" exclaimed Timothy.

Everyone in the room stood stock still and stared at her. The room grew bitter silent.

"It's my nightmare," Anna whispered to herself. "This is where I always wake up. I'm waking up. I'm waking up."

A moan escaped the object in her arms, and she recognized who it was. She wrapped her arms around the boy. He moaned as she held him close. "Colsson, are you okay?" she whispered in a frightened voice.

"Anna?" he whimpered in disbelief.

Realization hit Anna. She knew why she thought she'd seen the Smiths before. *She'd seen them in her nightmare!* She also realized that this time, she was *not* going to wake up.

Anna laid her hand on his back. His back was wet and sticky. She pulled her hand away and looked at it. It was blood!

Chapter Eleven

Esau stood in front of Anna. "What are you doing here?" he asked in a low, threatening tone. He bent down, snatched the limp, weak boy from Anna's arms, and pushed Colsson to the floor behind him.

"How did you get here?" Saul roared.

Remaining on the floor, she looked from one person to the next, too scared to speak. She felt her skin suddenly chill from the cold of the miserable underground room.

Esau grabbed her by the arm. "Are you deaf?" he yelled. His voice echoed off the walls, making the place seem even more eerie.

Before she could reply, Colsson cried out, "Leave her alone!" He pushed himself up and darted quickly in between Esau and Anna.

"Colsson, don't!" Anna begged.

He stood still in front of Esau.

Saul and Timothy came to stand on either side of Esau.

"Don't you dare hurt her!" Colsson growled through clenched teeth.

"Move out of the way before I kill you," Timothy snapped.

Anna's gaze saw Colsson's back as he stood above her. His dark blue shirt bore a deep, almost black, red tint. His whole back was completely covered in blood! Her gaze fell on Timothy's right side. He held a whip coiled in his hand.

Horror raced through her as the truth hit her. Colsson was being flogged! "Colsson, they'll kill you!" she cried as she jumped to her feet.

He turned to face her. "Anna, why are you here?"

"I was trying to get home—"

Crack! Colsson's whole body jerked, and he threw his head back in agony. He emitted a cry and fell to the floor.

"Colsson!" Anna yelled. She knelt next to him, wishing she knew what to do and praying for help.

"Timothy, don't hurt the girl!" Polly cried from where she stood.

Anna felt a rough hand on her arm right as Polly was speaking. The hand left her, and Timothy went to Polly and brought the coiled whip down on her shoulder. Polly gave a little cry as she cowered.

"That will teach you to tell me what to do," her husband growled.

"Dad, what do we do with her?" asked Esau, pointing at Anna.

Timothy came to stand by his son again, his hands on his hips. "What are you doing here?" he asked harshly.

"I was trying to get home," she stammered. "I got lost."

"A likely story," Saul snorted.

"That's the truth," said Anna, fury building inside her. "And when I get back, I'll tell my father and Deputy Sanders where you are, and they'll come get you."

Her words hit home. Polly still stood shaking in the corner. Saul, Esau, and Timothy whispered amongst themselves.

Colsson lay on the floor where he had fallen, the last stroke having weakened him past the point of standing.

"Anna," Colsson whispered. "Anna, get out of here."

"But they'll kill you if I leave. I can't possibly get help and make it back in time. I can't risk it."

He supported himself on an elbow. With his other hand, he firmly held Anna's chin and made her look him in the eye. "Anna, listen to me. I don't care what happens to me, but you cannot stay here. Get out of here. Now."

Colsson's new attitude scared Anna. He was commanding her to leave. What should she do?

"I can't leave you," she whispered, tears springing to her eyes.

He grabbed her by the arm and shook it. "If you stay, they'll not only kill me, but they'll kill you too." A tear dripped down his cheek, and he held her chin again. "I am telling you to leave because I *love* you."

Anna wrapped her arms around him, bloody back and all. She let him go and ran up the stairs, blinded by her tears. As she ran out the shack, she could hear angry voices behind her. Heavy footsteps on the stairs behind her thudded as loudly as her racing heart. She ran to Emerald and mounted. But before she could ride away, Saul came charging after her. He caught Emerald by the halter and yanked Anna off.

She screamed and struggled to get away from Saul, but she couldn't. He held her arms behind her back and forced her inside the shack and down to the cellar.

"I caught her, Dad," Saul said before he had reached the end of the stairs.

Esau stood in front of the exit after Saul brought her into the cellar.

Colsson was in the middle of the room. Timothy stood above him, whip uncurled.

"Please don't hurt him anymore!" Anna begged tearfully.

Saul jerked her. "Shut up," he growled. "He won't tell us everything he told you."

"But maybe he will now that we have her," said Timothy. He came to stand in front of Anna, whip in hand. "We can use her to our advantage."

"Perhaps," said Esau, his arms crossed and an evil sneer on his face.

"Or," said Timothy, "he'll talk as long as we promise not to hurt her. If he doesn't, I have the power to end her life same as I do with him."

"If we do anything to her, we'll be in prison for the rest of our lives," said Saul.

"We'll end up in prison anyway if Colsson doesn't tell us everything he told them," said Timothy. He crossed over to Colsson and brought the whip down across the boy's back with a resounding, blood-churning *snap!* "If we don't find out what was told, how are we supposed to find a way out of this mess?"

"Let him alone," Polly begged from the corner. "The law enforcement is going to find out what is really happening sooner or later. If only you hadn't had this hate in your soul, we *wouldn't* be in this 'mess'."

"Shut up, Polly!" Timothy shouted. "It's his own fault he won't tell. He's going to pay for it."

"But what do we do now?" asked Esau. "With her here, it complicates everything. When Campbell finds out his daughter is missing, he's going to go over the ranch and the territory beyond with a fine-toothed comb until he finds her. What then?"

Timothy called the twins to him. Saul let Anna go. She tried to run to Colsson, but Timothy stepped in front of her.

"Don't you dare try to escape," Timothy growled. "If you do..." He cracked his whip to complete the threat.

Anna shuddered and cowered. Timothy turned his back on her and gathered Polly and the twins in a close group.

While they whispered to each other, Anna crawled to Colsson.

"You've gone through this before, haven't you?"

Colsson had his fists clenched in pain. "Yes," he choked. "Many times before."

"How did you survive?"

"I did, somehow. I've always had to be careful because the scars break open very easily. Remember when we rushed home after you took me to the treehouse for the first time?"

She nodded. "You were very anxious to get home."

"Butterscotch's trotting caused some of the more fragile scars to break. My back felt sweaty, but I wasn't so sure it was sweat. When you weren't watching, I checked, and I was right. It was blood. I rubbed it off my hands the best I could with dust."

"And that's why you didn't want me to touch you."

"Yes. Mostly because it was very painful, but I also didn't want you to find out about the blood."

"Colsson, you should have told me your back was bleeding. I could have done something to help, and I would have taken it upon myself to call the sheriff instead of trying to talk to my parents." She paused. "I didn't even think about calling the sheriff myself. I should have done that weeks ago."

"I wasn't willing to tell you about everything. I didn't want you to know about this part."

"What about the sheets I found with blood on them?" she asked, remembering her thoughts when she found the red grass.

"Some of the scars broke in the night," Colsson said simply. "The sheets were spread out on the floor for me to sleep on, then hidden. They didn't know about the blood, or they would have panicked. They didn't really think anybody would find the sheets, either."

"Can you get out of your shirt?" Anna asked. "I'll try to stop the bleeding if I can."

He gritted his teeth and raised himself partially off the floor.

She felt almost sick, but she eased the shirt off.

He sucked in his breath as he lowered himself back down to the floor.

"Colsson, it's going to hurt, but I'm going to try to slow the bleeding," she whispered.

He nodded and groaned.

"God, please help me," Anna murmured to herself as she lay the cleaner side of the shirt against his back. She dreaded what she had to do next. A wave of dizziness swept over her. She looked at her arms and hands, already bloody from hugging him before. She held her breath and braced herself.

Blood oozed between her fingers and made a strange, sucking sound as she put light pressure down on the shirt.

Colsson squeezed his eyes shut, yanked his knee toward his chest, and cried aloud, startling his family into turning around.

Esau rushed forward to stop Anna, but Timothy held out his arm. "Let her alone. It won't do her much good. If she can stop the bleeding, all her efforts will be for nothing. I'm tired of Colsson not telling us."

Dread and fear shot through Colsson.

Occupied with her thoughts and prayers, Anna did not hear Timothy.

"Anna," Colsson whispered.

"Yes, Colsson?"

"Yesterday afternoon, you were telling me about a place you go if you are evil?"

"Hell," Anna replied.

"Tell me what the other place is like."

"It is a place where there is no sorrow, no fear, and no pain. I cannot even begin to imagine what it looks like."

"How long do you have there?"

"As I told you yesterday, you have a choice between suffering forever or living in joy and peace with the Lord forever."

"What must I do to go there?"

"Paradise?"

"Yes," he replied softly.

"Surrender completely to the Lord, repent of every sin you've committed, and beg His forgiveness."

"What does 'repent' mean?" asked Colsson.

"Realize what you have done, admit you've done it, and be truly sorry for it."

Tears of regret ran down his cheeks. "How can God forgive someone who's hated Him for as long as I have?"

A tear slipped down Anna's face, a grateful tear. He was preparing to come to the Lord! "When Christ was crucified, He paid the price for *all* our sins, so that we only had to believe, and trust Him, and have faith in Him, and He would take us to be with Him in heaven."

"Crucified?"

"In Christ's time, criminals were killed brutally. They were nailed to a cross, alive, and they died a slow, agonizing death. A cross is a giant t-shape made of wood. It was the most awful way to die, I think. Jesus Christ was whipped, as you have been, but perhaps much worse, and He was nailed to a cross, though He had never sinned."

"They put nails *through* him?" he asked in horror.

Anna nodded. "They did that to hold Him to the cross. He died on that cross, and He was buried in a tomb that had never been used before. Then, three days later, a miracle happened. Christ came to life again."

"Even though He was dead? How is that possible?"

"Anything is possible with God. Jesus is God's Son. So, He is God."

"But if He was God, how could He die?"

"It happened for the sake of saving the world. He died to save us so we could *all* live with Him in heaven if only we would ask His forgiveness and believe in Him."

"But, even if I asked, would God forgive someone who has hated Him all his life?"

She took a deep breath. "When Christ was crucified, He was nailed to the cross between two thieves, one at His right and one at His left. One thief cursed Jesus and mocked Him along with many others. The other thief came to Jesus' defense and then said, 'Lord, remember me.' Jesus told that thief, a dirty criminal guilty enough to be killed on a cross, 'I tell you the truth, today you will be with Me in Paradise.'"

"He forgave a thief? A criminal? Who has that kind of love?"

"God does," Anna whispered softly. "He loves each of us far beyond anything we could ever imagine. He will also forgive you, Colsson, if only you ask Him to. He loves you that much."

He bit his lip. "Anna, I have to tell you something. I don't want to, but I want you to be ready and know what's going to happen."

Anna pulled the shirt away from his back, relieved to see the bleeding had slowed. For the first time, Anna saw the scars covering his back. There was not a healthy patch of flesh anywhere. "What is it you want to tell me?" she asked as she examined the scars more closely. She traced one with her finger. What his family had done to him was horrifying.

"They're going to kill me, Anna," he whispered, choking.

Anna quickly turned her head to see his face. "No, they won't," she whispered in horror. "I won't let them. They can't!"

"They can, and they will. They said so a few minutes ago."

"But I didn't hear them say that!"

"I did. He's going to flog me to death. You won't have a choice as to stay or leave. Please don't watch. Close your eyes and turn away."

She squeezed his shoulder, terrified. "Please God," she whispered. "Spare his life."

His hand found hers. "Anna, it's over. My life is over."

"But you can't let them!" Anna burst into tears. "I've never cared about anyone like I have you! Pray the Lord will save you. Don't give up now."

"You have already helped my life to be spared," he whispered as he painfully rolled to his side. He tenderly put his hand on the side of Anna's face. "I know now where I am going. Because of you. You showed me just how much Christ loves us. Me." His voice dropped even lower. "I only wish I could see you again."

"You will," Anna murmured. Helplessness filled her. Colsson was right. "I believe we will see each other again."

"Remember that I love you more than anything on this earth," he whispered softly as he wrapped his arms around her. He squeezed his eyes shut and tried to hide his fierce agony as her arms clung to his back.

"I'm going to miss you so much," she whispered, barely audible. She hugged him hard. "I could never care more about a human being more than I care about you."

He let her go, and he again laid his clammy hand on the side of her face.

She put her blood-covered hand on top of his. She struggled to choke out words through her gentle weeping. "I love you."

The words barely left her mouth when one of the twins jerked her away from Colsson. She fought back. "Let me go!" she cried, tears still pouring down her face. Despair filled her. Colsson didn't have long to live. She loved him so much. How could God take him away from her?

Esau left Anna in the corner of the room. Anna tried to chase after him, praying she might still be able to save Colsson. She felt a gentle hand on her shoulder.

Tears glistened in Polly's eyes. "There's nothing you can do," she whispered. "If you try to save him, you will only be beaten to death also. I have tried, and never succeeded."

Polly put her arms around the grief-stricken girl. Anna laid her head on Polly's shoulder and cried without restraint. With all her heart, Anna longed to and tried to make herself go to Colsson, no matter what happened to her. But something held her back. Try though she may, she stood rooted in place.

Anger kindled inside her. God didn't care about how she felt! How could He when He was taking away the only person she ever truly loved? Loved. She had grown to love Colsson with all her heart, and now she would never be allowed to love him as she truly did. "God, why? Why are you doing this? You know how much I love him, how much he means to me."

Timothy, Saul, and Esau stood around Colsson. Timothy uncoiled his whip, anger boiling inside him that Colsson would not tell him what he wanted to know. Saul and Esau stood with their arms crossed, the same thoughts as their father filling their minds.

Through her tears, Anna saw Colsson awaiting the blows. His eyes were closed, and his lips moved, praying what Anna had told him to.

"ANNA," God whispered. "REMEMBER THAT HE HAS COME TO ME, AND THAT IS THE MOST IMPORTANT THING. NO MATTER WHAT HAPPENS, LOVE WILL ALWAYS REMAIN. LOVE HIM EVEN IF HE IS GONE. LOVE HIM EVEN IF HE STAYS. LOVE IS SOMETHING I WON'T EVER TAKE AWAY FROM SOMEONE. LET YOUR MIND REST. I HAVE A GREATER PLAN IN MIND."

Crack! The tip of the whip ripped Colsson's back, and pain shot through his entire body. Colsson's cry followed the violent snap.

Anna jumped as though she were the one who had received the lash. Her head remained on Polly's shoulder.

Again and again, the whip snapped, and again and again, Colsson cried after each lash.

Anna turned her head slightly to see Colsson. The boy writhed in agony on the floor, his face contorted, and fierce cries escaped his throat. Every stroke lacerated his scars and blood splurted from the wounds as soon as they were cut. Extreme pain circulated through his entire body. Tears of agony poured down his face. Blood poured off his back and pooled on the ground.

Anna wailed aloud. A bittersweet love filled her to the end. "God, how can I just stand here when Colsson is dying?"

"REMEMBER ME. HE HAS BEEN SAVED, AND HE WILL LIVE IN ETERNITY WITH ME IN MY GOOD TIME. BE STILL, AND KNOW I AM GOD."

Anna closed her eyes. She lifted her head from Polly's shoulder. Polly didn't dare look at Colsson. Tears trickled silently down her aged cheeks.

Choking over the tears yet unshed, Anna forced herself to turn her gaze to the boy writhing on the ground. She looked just in time to see the whip tear Colsson's chest. Hate coated Timothy's face as he violently struck Colsson repeatedly.

Polly listened to Anna praying. Her heart trembled within her. "Lord, I believe," she whispered. "I believe again. I was lost, but You have brought me back."

"Dad, he's dead," Esau announced.

Timothy stopped cold. "He's dead?" he whispered hoarsely.

"He's not moving anymore," Saul replied.

"Oh no," Timothy panicked. "He can't be!" The whip fell from his hand. "I didn't even lash him enough to kill him!"

"Personally, I'm glad he's out of our way," Saul said boldly. He and Esau left the basement.

Anna and Polly couldn't tear their eyes away from where Colsson lay sprawled on the ground. Blood coated the ground next to him where it had gushed free as soon as the tip of the whip had ripped his back.

Anna slowly left Polly, gaze transfixed on Colsson.

Polly bowed her head and sank to the floor against the wall. "He rests in peace," she whispered to herself. "With God. God will take away all his distress, pain, and tears. He will give Colsson peace, and justice to those who dare be as cruel to him as this."

Anna knelt next to Colsson and touched his cheek. "Colsson," she whispered. Her vision blurred. Inconsolably, she wailed.

Chapter Twelve

Timothy sank down on the steps and hid his face in his hands. "I never truly intended to kill him," he murmured to himself. He lifted his head. His cruel heart tore in two when he saw Anna crying next to Colsson. Instantly he was taken back to the day Kelly was killed.

He remembered his pain he had felt in his heart when he saw Kelly, dead in his car. He loved Kelly dearly, and when Kelly was killed, he wanted to torture the Helders, the family involved in the accident, to show them what the pain was like and to leave behind his own pain. He adopted Colsson Helder for that purpose.

Wearily, Anna slipped her hand into Colsson's hand. She felt his fingers move ever so slightly, numbly. Anna emitted a frightened scream. She jerked her hand away and pushed herself to her feet, eyes fixated on his body. He didn't move, didn't flinch.

"What? What is it?" cried Polly.

"He moved!" were the only words that Anna could say. She pointed to him.

Timothy slowly rose and went to Colsson. He felt Colsson's throat. "It was just reflexes," he choked. "He's gone."

Anna was startled to hear Timothy's soft tone. This wasn't the Timothy she knew!

Timothy felt her staring at him. He turned to face her, tears in his eyes. "I never meant to kill him," he told her. "I promise you, I never meant to kill him. He was weaker than I ever realized, to die so soon."

Anna could only gape at Timothy.

Timothy took a couple steps toward her, and she took a step back. He stopped. "I never meant to kill him," he repeated.

"You didn't kill me," came a voice from behind Timothy. Everyone spun toward the voice in disbelief.

Colsson had rolled to his side and was supporting himself on his arms. He kept his eyes down.

Anna's jaw dropped. "Colsson!" she shrieked. "You were dead!"

"But...but I didn't feel a pulse!" Timothy stammered.

Before anyone knew what was happening, Colsson slumped over again.

"What should we do?" Polly cried.

"Get him back to the ranch as fast as we can," Timothy replied determinedly. "Saul! Esau! Get down here!"

The twins thundered down the stairs.

"Colsson's alive!" said Timothy. "We've got to get him back as quick as we can. Help us out."

The twins stared with confusion at Timothy. What had come over him?

"Don't just stand there! Saul, run as fast as you can to the car and get something to slow the bleeding. Do you remember where we hid the car?"

Saul nodded, "Yes, but—"

"No buts. Get moving!"

Saul ran out of the basement, dazed with confusion. What was going on? Why did his father so suddenly want to keep Colsson alive? "I thought Dad would sooner have let Colsson die!"

Back at the shack, Timothy commanded, "Esau, you help me carry him out and to the car."

"Wait!" cried Anna. "Emerald is outside. She can take him to the car a whole lot faster."

Timothy nodded. "Okay, we'll use the horse. Polly, you're the lightest, you go on the horse with Colsson. We have to wait for Saul to get back before we get him on."

Timothy and Esau carried Colsson's limp form out of the shack and laid him face down in front of it.

"Hurry, Saul!" Timothy anxiously whispered to himself.

Anna grabbed Timothy by the arm and said, "Timothy, don't take him to the ranch. Take him straight to the Meadowbrook emergency room. It'll be faster than going to the ranch first."

Timothy soberly held her hand close to him. "Do you trust me?"

Anna bit her lip and dropped her eyes before looking back up. "No," she murmured.

"I won't fail you. I solemnly swear. I see how much you love him. When I saw that love you have for him, I was reminded of how much I loved someone no longer with us. Something broke inside me when I realized there is pain beside my own."

"Take care of him," Anna choked as she fought to keep her fear and tears inside.

Timothy nodded. "You'll meet us there, won't you?"

"I will head back home and tell my parents. We'll join you there," Anna replied.

Just then, Saul arrived, out of breath and clutching cloth. "Several...of his...sh—shirts," he panted.

Timothy snatched the shirts from Saul and immediately pressed them against Colsson's back, like Anna had done earlier.

Timothy ripped off his belt, commanding Saul and Esau to do the same. Using the belts, he fastened the layers of cloth to Colsson's back. "Get up on the horse, Polly!"

Anna helped Polly get up on Emerald's back. Then, Timothy, Saul, and Esau lifted Colsson up onto Emerald. Polly held onto Colsson with one arm and held the reins with her other hand.

"We'll be there as soon as we can," Timothy said.

Anna followed the three men through the woods. The Smiths had left their car in the brush as they could drive no further into the timbered land.

Polly had managed to get Colsson off Emerald and into the middle seat of the Suburban. The vehicle was started and ready to go.

A feeling of distrust came over Anna as the twins got into the back seats, and Timothy moved toward the driver's seat. What if it all was just an act? What if they didn't go to the hospital like they said they would?

"TAKE THE CHANCE. IT IS THE ONLY THING YOU CAN DO."

"We'll meet you at the hospital," Timothy called to Anna as she stood beside Emerald. "I only hope we can get him there in time."

Timothy drove away.

"Dad, what is going on?" asked Esau.

Timothy took a deep breath before answering. "I never meant to kill Colsson. I truly didn't."

"You sure acted like it," Saul remarked. He and Esau were leaning on the back of the middle seats, out of their own seats.

"I...I know I did," Timothy replied. "Hate is what did it. And, I think, pain."

"Pain?" Polly echoed softly in disbelief.

Timothy held his hand over his heart. "I still ache inside from losing Kelly. I miss Kelly terribly. Even after ten years. I can

148

never leave the pain behind. At times, the pain is worse than others. I need to do something to get the pain behind me. I go wild, and nearly killed Colsson.

"When I saw Anna crying next to Colsson, I was reminded of how I felt after Kelly died. I realized just how wrong I'd been in doing this. Hurting Colsson doesn't ease the pain like I used to think."

As they listened to Timothy, Saul and Esau's hearts slowly began to soften. Together, they sat back down.

"I...I never thought about it like that," Saul murmured.

Thoughts of Kelly filled the minds of the whole family.

Esau impatiently brushed at a tear. "What can we do?"

"Not much," Timothy admitted.

Anna watched the Smiths pull away. She turned to Emerald, but before she mounted, she caught sight of her arms and hands and groaned. "Mom and Dad will freak out if they see this blood on me." She knelt next to the brook and scrubbed at the blood the best she could, clenching her teeth as she splashed the freezing water over her arms.

Though tired, she swung herself onto Emerald's back when she was done and turned the mare to follow the brook. Colsson was still alive, but would he live to see the new day? Would he even make the journey to the hospital? Would the Smiths even take him there? The feeling of distrust came back, stronger than ever. She urged Emerald faster. She had to get to the hospital as soon as she could.

When Anna rode into the barnyard, Frank and Liesel were sitting in a couple chairs, obviously distraught. Frank had his chin resting in his hand and Liesel looked off into space. They rose from their chairs and walked to her. Liesel wrapped her arms around Anna as soon as she dismounted.

"You sure were gone a long time, honey," Liesel remarked.

"I didn't mean to wander off, Mom," Anna said. "I just didn't think, and I ended up going through the meadow instead of toward home."

"How did you go through the meadow instead of toward home?" asked Frank.

"I was thinking about Colsson, and how much I cared about him," Anna replied. "I was worried."

"We still don't know where he is," said Frank.

"The Smiths took him to the hospital," said Anna. "I found him while trying to get home. There's an old shack, a miner's shack I think, beyond the ranch's border a few miles. I heard screaming, and snapping, and I thought it was a mountain lion in the branches. I came upon the shack from the north. I heard Timothy yelling at the top of his lungs, asking Colsson what he told us."

"Why there?" asked Liesel.

"They must have come across it on one of their all-day trips," said Frank. "Then they went there to avoid being found by the law enforcement."

Anna resumed her story. "I went into the shack and had to go through a trapdoor because they were underground. When I reached the bottom of the stairs, I caught Colsson as Saul threw him across the room. It was my nightmare all over again, but this time it was *real*. In my dream, I felt the liquid, but didn't know what it was. Then, I found out. It was blood. Colsson's blood. Timothy Smith was *flogging* Colsson."

"Flogging?" Frank repeated in alarm.

"With a whip," said Anna. "His back was covered in blood." She paused and shuddered.

"Then what?" Frank pressed.

"The Smiths went into conference, and I tried to stop the bleeding. While I was helping Colsson, he came to the Lord."

"He did?" Liesel gave an excited shriek. "I remember he

wasn't a believer when he first came."

You believed me telling you that he wasn't a believer, but not that something was wrong, Anna thought to herself. "He told me he was going to be flogged to death."

Frank exhaled and hid his face in his hand. Liesel gasped. "Oh no!"

"One of the twins dragged me away from him. Timothy beat him until he no longer moved or cried in agony."

"Why didn't you try to get away?" Frank demanded.

"I did when Colsson told me to," Anna replied softly, "I couldn't get away. Saul caught me."

"He's on the way to the hospital, you said?" asked Frank.

Anna nodded. "Yes."

"We'd better get over there," said Frank. He stopped. "Wait, you said the *Smiths* are taking him to the hospital?"

"That's what they said, but somehow, Dad, I don't entirely trust them. Timothy seemed to regret beating Colsson so hard and said he never meant to kill Colsson. But..."

"I don't like it either," Frank declared. "Let's get over there and see if they're actually there."

When the Campbells reached the hospital, they searched the busy waiting room for the Smiths.

"There they are!" Liesel cried when she caught sight of the twins' red hair. "They *did* bring him here!"

The Campbells hurried over to where the Smiths sat.

Timothy stood. "I'm glad you're here. We haven't heard any news."

"Before you say anything more, Timothy, I want you to explain exactly what is going on," Frank said firmly.

Timothy nodded. "It's not easy, but I suppose I owe you all an explanation. Please sit down."

When the Campbells were seated, Timothy began, "Ten years ago, there was a severe car accident not far from our house. I ran all the way there to see what had happened when we heard the crash. When I got there, I saw a car I recognized, that of my son's. My oldest son, Kelly, was in the car. He was killed in the accident."

Timothy faltered. Frank leaned forward. "I'm sorry," he murmured.

Timothy regained his voice. "There was another vehicle involved in the wreck. A family by the name of Helder. The parents also were killed in the accident. Colsson's their son."

"You mean Colsson's not your son?" asked Liesel.

"We adopted him." Timothy hung his head. "Actually, there's a reason we adopted him. I—I convinced myself that the accident was the Helders' fault, and I wanted them to pay for Kelly's death. I was desperate to put my pain behind me. I thought that by abusing Colsson, I could forget it all. I became so angry, and the ache in my chest compelled me to be so frightfully terrible. I...I nearly killed Colsson because of it."

Deputy Sanders interrupted as he walked up to the group. "I'm afraid I have to take you to headquarters."

Polly, Saul, and Esau held their breaths, wondering what Timothy's reaction would be.

"I understand," said Timothy quietly.

Saul and Esau gaped. What a transformation that had come over their father!

A while after Deputy Sanders had escorted the Smiths out of the building, a doctor came out to talk to the Campbells.

"How is he?" asked Anna.

"We don't know for sure yet. He's had a rough time, and we don't expect him to live. He's lost too much blood. You're friends of his, correct?"

"Correct," replied Frank. He folded his arms over his chest.

He forced himself to speak strongly, struggling to hide the worry that came over him.

"In my entire career, I've never seen anyone who's received a flogging like he has. I believe it has proven fatal. We're running a blood test, then we'll try to do a transfusion and hope it's not too late. He's in shock, and his blood pressure is falling by the minute. He's one step away from irreversible shock which means there will be nothing we can do to save him. I'm surprised he has endured this long."

When the doctor left, Anna committed herself to prayer. "You've spared him till now," she whispered. "Please let him live."

Frank and Liesel also prayed consistently. For another hour, the Campbells prayed and waited until the doctor came out again. "We managed to do the transfusion, but it's not a guarantee to save his life."

"Okay. Thank you," said Frank, wearily.

The doctor continued, "Do you know about his younger years? Was he being abused then?"

"We don't know," Frank replied. "That's all I can figure."

"He told me he doesn't remember anything from his childhood," said Anna.

The doctor stroked his chin. "That's helpful to know. I'll check into that. Thank you."

"We'll come back tomorrow," said Frank.

"Please do that," the doctor replied.

"Oh, I hope he's not too scared here all alone," Anna murmured.

The doctor bit his lip. "He's most likely not going to regain consciousness for a long time. If—" He stopped.

"If he does at all," Frank finished softly. After a moment of silence, Frank said, "We'll be back."

Frank led Anna and Liesel out of the hospital.

Chapter Thirteen

That night, no sleep came to Anna. Worry and fear for Colsson's life haunted her. Her sheets became more twisted each time she tossed and turned. The doctor's and her father's words tormented her mind.

"He's most likely not going to regain consciousness for a long time. If—"

"If he does at all."

For the hundredth time, those words echoed in her head. "God, I beg you, please be with him tonight. Please let him live. Give him strength, give him healing. Please remind me of love, Your love. Remind me that You haven't abandoned Colsson. Please show him Your love. Let him see it, and understand."

After breakfast the next morning, the Campbells went to the hospital again. Weary from no sleep the previous night, Anna tried to sleep a little on the way to the hospital.

At the hospital, Frank asked the desk nurse for Colsson's room number. The Campbells made their way to the room.

When Frank knocked on the door, a nurse came out.

"How is he?" Frank whispered.

"He's not doing very well," the nurse replied. "He was in the ICU all last night. He's regained consciousness, but he's very frightened. He keeps calling for an Anna."

Anna didn't say anything, but her heart jumped.

"Is he conscious right now?" asked Frank.

155

"Barely," the nurse replied. "You're welcome to go in if you want."

"Thank you."

Frank held the door open for Anna and Liesel. Liesel let Anna go through first. Anna passed through the doorway and went straight, but slowly, to Colsson's bedside. His eyes were closed, and his hand rested on his chest. She touched his shoulder. "Colsson?" she whispered softly.

He stirred slightly.

"Colsson, can you hear me?"

Colsson's eyes opened slowly. Anna moved her hand down his arm and slipped her hand into his. Colsson's fingers stirred as they tried to close around her hand. His eyes closed again. "Anna?" he murmured.

Anna brushed a strand of his hair away from his forehead. "It's all over, just as I told you it would be."

Strength gone, no reply passed his lips though he tried.

Liesel and Frank looked at each other, then left the room.

Anna knelt next to the bed and his eyes opened slightly. He was pale, and he could barely move at all. "It's...over?" he murmured, his voice a weak and strained whisper, and he struggled to speak.

She nodded. "They won't ever hurt you again." She gently laid her hand on his forehead.

Relief and peace surged through him. He tried to squeeze her hand again, but he could barely move his fingers and immediately gave up.

"Thank...you...God," he murmured. His eyes remained closed. His lips moved as his head sank farther into his pillow.

Anna also thanked the Father that his abuse was over. She stroked his blond hair back and let him rest for a few minutes.

The nurse came and made her routine check as she spoke quietly to Anna.

"You seem to have a calming effect on him," she remarked to Anna. "He's scared to death of us. This is the first time I've come in and he hasn't struggled."

"I think he's sleeping right now," Anna replied.

"That's what I mean. I come in, barely touch him, and he wakes up. He tries to get away, but he can barely move. He's already improved a little since I last checked him."

Anna smiled. "He's a friend of mine. I was the only one he told about what was happening to him."

"I think he trusts you. He feels safe now that you're here. If you stayed here more, he might get better more quickly."

"May I ask why he isn't lying face down?" Anna changed the subject, concern taking over her thoughts.

"We did. We tried. Whenever he was conscious face down, he thrashed around, thinking he was going to get beaten again. That thrashing caused some of the scars to break open and trying to hold him down just made it worse. We hated to, but we had to lay him on his back. At least he's not going to try to move. It's risky, but we couldn't deal with him lying face down. We didn't have a choice."

"I understand," Anna murmured. A tingle went down her spine. "Isn't it extremely painful for him though?"

"It is painful, but we have him on a strong pain medication." The nurse smiled. "Your parents are walking around outside. They asked me to tell you." Looking satisfied that everything was finished, she left.

Anna turned her attention back to Colsson. He stirred. She caressed his face under his eye with her finger. "Hey," she said quietly and softly. "How're you doing?"

His eyes slowly flickered open. She gently squeezed his shoulder. He groaned as he struggled to wake up.

"Try not to move," she said gently as he squirmed. She held his shoulders to the bed and he stopped instantly. "You'll tear scars."

He exhaled. "I'm glad you're here. I'm frightened of this hospital."

"I know," she whispered. "I don't think you'll have to stay here much longer. Then you can come back to the ranch with us. Everybody's working very hard so you can."

"Why can't we go now?"

"The doctors haven't released you yet. They'll have to keep you here for a little while longer until you can survive without them. You had a rough time yesterday, Colsson."

"But I don't want to be here. You speak of it as though I'm a prisoner here."

Anna could have kicked herself. The last thing he needed was a reminder of his cruel, past life. Even though she had used simple terms used all the time for this sort of thing, it would only scare Colsson all the more.

"What are they going to do to me?" Colsson asked tensely. He lifted his head and looked into her eyes, scared.

Anna squeezed his hand. "I'm sorry. I shouldn't have said those things about releasing you and keeping you here. That's just what everybody says when they talk about staying longer in the hospital. They won't hurt you, Colsson. You're safe, I promise."

Colsson let his head go back down to the pillow. The fear in his eyes eased little.

"How're you feeling?"

"I hurt all over, but mostly my back. It's torture laying on my back."

"Would you rather be on your stomach? I know there are scars and wounds on your chest, but they're fewer than on your back."

"No," he replied firmly. "I can't be on my stomach. Every time someone approaches me I keep thinking—"

Anna put her hand over Colsson's mouth, cutting him off. "I understand. Don't talk about it now."

Knock, knock. Someone rapped on the door.

"Come in," Anna called.

The door opened, and a young man came into the room. He was tall and lean, but he had an athletic build and broad shoulders. He had blond hair. His gentle, blue eyes watched Colsson as he closed the door behind him. "Colsson?" he murmured.

"Who are you?" asked Colsson.

The young man went to the other side of the bed. "Colsson."

Colsson drew back from the young man.

As though choked, the young man whispered, "I won't hurt you, Colsson. I thought I'd never see you again." Gently, strongly, the young man put his arms around the injured boy and hugged him tightly, fighting to keep tears inside. "I thought I'd never see you again."

Colsson cried out in pain and fear. He struggled to tear away.

The young man released Colsson. Tears welled in the stranger's eyes when Colsson looked at him with distrust. "Colsson, don't you remember me? It's me, Walt!"

"I don't know who you are," said Colsson.

Walt backed off slightly. "What do you mean?"

"Who are you? What are you doing?"

Walt couldn't stop the tears now. Defeated, he sank into a chair next to the bed. "We swore we wouldn't ever forget each other! How do you not know me?"

Colsson turned pleading eyes to Anna.

"But I'm your brother. We were separated when we were boys."

"You're related to Colsson?" Anna asked in disbelief.

"Yes, I'm Walt Helder and this is Colsson Helder, my brother." He wiped his eyes.

"Brother?" Colsson repeated, squinting at Walt. "But Saul and Esau—"

A voice jumped in. "He suffered a head injury a long time ago, Walt. That's probably why he doesn't remember you."

They all turned to look at the doctor who had entered the room. He wasn't the same one who had talked to the Campbells the night before.

You'll have to give him time. We found that old head injury last night. It looks as though he suffered a Grade 1 concussion and had retrograde amnesia. And in the car accident, his skull was fractured."

"*That's* why you didn't remember anything from your childhood, Colsson," said Anna. "Now it makes sense."

The doctor came to Anna and put out his hand. "I'm Dr. Trooper."

Walt had his face hidden in his hands. His shoulders shook. Muffled sobbing escaped his throat.

Dr. Trooper went to Walt and put squeezed his shoulder.

"I just want my brother back, Dad," Walt cried.

"Give him time. He may remember if you help him. I'll see you later."

Anna was confused. Dad? If Walt was Colsson's brother, then Dr. Trooper must have adopted Walt after the accident.

"Tell me the story, Walt," said Colsson. "What is it? I don't remember anything."

Walt lifted his face and rubbed his red eyes. "When our mom and dad hadn't been married for very long, Mom was pregnant with me. When I was a couple years old, Mom was pregnant again with you. Mom and Dad loved us very much, and our family was always close. We had a wonderful family."

"What happened?" asked Colsson.

"When you were nine and I was twelve, we were in a bad car accident." Walt hesitated. "Mom and Dad were killed. You and I were the only survivors."

Walt hid his face in his hands, shaken by the reminiscence. "I kept trying to wake Mom and Dad by yelling for them, but they didn't answer. You and I were saved, but they couldn't save Mom and Dad."

"Somehow that story seems familiar," Colsson murmured.

"That's because it was real," said Walt.

"That's awful," Colsson said softly. He tried to turn toward Walt but gasped and groaned with pain. He gave up with a sigh and let his head return to the pillow.

"We were put into a foster care, which was not a good one. Then, the Smiths came to adopt you, but they didn't want me. We promised never to forget each other. It was a very sad goodbye. Both of us were heartbroken. When they took you away, I swore I would find you again somehow. "

Memories flooded Colsson's mind. All of a sudden, he could picture that day when he and Walt were separated. Their tearful goodbyes, the Smiths cruelly dragging him away. Memories of his real parents came back, and of the times their family had together. When he looked at Walt again, recognition—beautiful recognition—came instantly. No longer did he see Walt as a stranger, but the brother he remembered being taken away from.

Something else came to mind. A replay of an incident formed before his mind's eye. Timothy, holding on to him and shaking him. Wrestling him near the side of an outbuilding. Bashing his head against the building. He moaned and slumped down to the ground. Pain split through his head. The world spun and confusion took hold.

Colsson winced and touched his head, feeling again the pain

he had felt so long ago.

"I remember the day I lost my memory," he said softly. "It's not very clear, but I remember Timothy bashing my head against the side of a building. That's how it happened." He looked up. "And I remember you."

Anna tiptoed out of the room. Her parents were just returning, so she walked up to them.

"What are you doing?" asked Liesel.

"I'm letting Walt have some time alone with Colsson."

"*Who?*" Frank lifted an eyebrow.

"Colsson has a brother he didn't remember. One of the doctors here adopted him soon after the Smiths adopted Colsson."

"A brother?" asked Frank. "Timothy didn't mention Colsson having a brother."

"No, he didn't," Anna said thoughtfully.

"Why didn't the Smiths adopt Walt too?" asked Frank.

Anna shrugged. "I don't know. Walt said they didn't want him, but—" she paused as a thought struck her. "Maybe the Smiths separated them to increase the hurt."

"I never thought of that," said Frank.

"It makes sense, though," Liesel remarked. "I wouldn't put it past them to have done it."

"So, Walt is a Helder also?" asked Frank for confirmation.

Anna nodded. "Colsson had a head injury from abuse and probably the accident so he didn't remember anything from his childhood, including Walt. It broke Walt's heart to find out Colsson had forgotten him, but I think Colsson remembers him now."

"What does his brother look like?" asked Liesel. "Do they look anything alike?"

"They look similar," Anna replied. "Walt isn't skinny, but

their faces are similar, and they both have blond hair."

Liesel changed the subject. "How is Colsson doing?"

"He's terrified of the doctors, nurses, and the hospital, but he's okay when I'm here. Walt is keeping his mind occupied for the moment. It's only a matter of time before his fear returns."

"We have to go home pretty soon," said Frank. "Your mother has to start lunch for the boarders. Did you want to stay here?"

"My being here seems to be the only thing that will ease his mind. I can grab something to eat in the cafeteria."

Frank put an arm around Liesel and Anna and prayed aloud, begging for Colsson's healing. Anna struggled to keep tears from falling down her cheeks and dripping off her nose. Several times during the prayer, she took a shaky breath and swiped her face with her fingertips. After her parents left, she wandered toward the cafeteria. Her thoughts fixed purely on Colsson, she barely heard the voices and people surrounding her. She saw Dr. Trooper about to leave. He stopped to talk to her.

"Is Walt still in Colsson's room?"

"I believe he is," Anna replied.

"I'm the one who adopted Walt after Colsson was adopted."

Anna nodded and smiled. "I figured."

"When I adopted him, Walt was still heartbroken over losing his brother, and he wouldn't talk much. He didn't want to be with us, he just wanted his family back."

"That must have been awful for him," Anna murmured.

"We found out last night that Colsson was Colsson Helder. Same last name as Walt's. I remembered all Walt told me about his brother. After my colleagues and I were fairly certain Colsson would survive, I got permission to tell Walt about him. I will never forget last night for as long as I live. I've never seen Walt so full of hope, of joy. He broke down and cried when I told him. I even choked right then, and still do when I relive it in my mind."

"I can only imagine what it must have been like," said Anna.

Dr. Trooper chuckled with recollection. "Walt was so desperate to see his brother, he wanted to come to the hospital last night. I told him he could be at the hospital today, and wait until I told him he could see Colsson."

"He was crushed when Colsson didn't remember him."

"I know he was. I didn't know about the head injury until a little while ago, or I'd have warned Walt. I came to find him as soon as I found out, but it was too late."

"Colsson remembers him now. Walt is helping him remember parts of his childhood."

Dr. Trooper looked at his watch. "I have to get back to work. Have a good day."

"Thank you, you too," said Anna as Dr. Trooper moved on.

When Anna returned to Colsson's room, Walt was talking about things that had happened before their parents had died. Colsson was plainly exhausted from Walt's eagerness to reclaim his brother.

Anna went to the side of the bed and squeezed his shoulder. "You better rest for now, Colsson."

Walt stood. "I'll come back later. He's told me about you."

Anna smiled. "He has, has he?"

Walt left, but not before promising Colsson he would be back later. Anna knelt next to the bed and rested her folded arms on the edge.

Colsson barely had the strength to talk anymore. Mostly, he had been listening to Walt tell of the times before the accident. He closed his eyes.

"Anna," he murmured. "Stay with me...please..."

Anna picked up his hand. "I won't leave this room until you wake up."

He tried to say more but couldn't. His breathing evened as he drifted into a quiet and peaceful sleep.

Throughout the day, Anna waited and watched as Colsson slept on. She paced through the room swinging her arms, sat and looked out the window, and did as many things as she could to pass the time. Prayer was on her lips without fail.

Only when the sun and the horizon met did Colsson stir. Anna turned away from the window to see what he was doing. His eyes looked up at her.

"Hey, how're you doing?"

"Anna," he called weakly.

"I'm right here." She knelt next to the bed and laid her hand on his arm to let him know she was there.

"I want to go home."

"We can't take you home yet, Colsson," Anna murmured. She squeezed his hand. "I'm sorry."

"I don't want to be here anymore."

"I know you don't, but there's nothing we can do. We have to wait. You almost died, and they want to make sure it won't happen again. They are trying to help you."

"Put your arm around my shoulders, and stay here for a while," he pleaded.

Carefully so as not to wreck the scars and wounds on his back, Anna slid her arm under his upper back and squeezed his shoulder tight. Colsson lay his head back and closed his eyes. With her other hand, Anna pulled the blanket farther up, closer to his neck. Softly, she ran her fingers through his blond hair.

Anna stayed where she was for long after the sun left the sky. Colsson slept, his chest rising and falling evenly. The despair in his face had vanished, and ease and calmness replaced it.

Her arm nearly gone numb, she eased her arm out from under him. She rubbed her arm to get the blood flowing again.

Dr. Trooper came in a few minutes later to check Colsson.

"When can he go home?" she asked as he worked.

"We hope we can let him go in a few days," he whispered. "We're keeping a very close eye on him right now. He's stable for now, but if anything happened, it could be fatal. Plus, if we let him go now, he's going to be in pretty bad pain. He won't be able to move very easily. He may need physical therapy to prevent the scarring from hindering his abilities."

Anna nodded. "I understand, it's just that he's so terrified here. He feels like a prisoner, and I'm worried something might happen."

"That's understandable. If necessary, we can give him a tranquilizer to calm him down."

"That's helpful to know," Anna admitted.

"Walt's been pretty anxious all day long, but I told him he'd best not go in until he's fully awake. I understand he will go home with your family when he leaves here. Could Walt visit him at your ranch after he leaves here?"

"Of course," Anna replied. "I'll give you our phone number and you or Walt can call us."

Dr. Trooper wrote the number down.

"I better go call my parents, and have them come to the hospital," Anna excused herself.

When the Campbells came to the hospital to get Colsson a few days later, Dr. Trooper was there to talk to them. He discussed Colsson's current medical condition, his medications, and the follow-up care he required. He showed Anna and Liesel how to change the bandages covering his back and chest and how to care for the scars and wounds.

When they arrived outside with Colsson in a wheelchair, Frank helped him stand. In weakness, Colsson nearly collapsed. Frank tightened his grip on Colsson and pulled him back up. "Go slow, Colsson," he encouraged gently. "One step at a time."

Regaining a little strength with each step, by the time they had left the building, Frank hardly had to support him at all. Right before they reached the vehicle, he stopped.

"Frank, please let me go the rest of the way. I want to know I can."

Frank withdrew his arm. Colsson expelled his breath and took a shaky step. Slowly, he managed to walk the few steps to the vehicle door. He seemed exhausted but proud of himself for his accomplishment.

Anna helped Colsson settle into his bed in the ranch house. Short grunts of effort escaped his throat as he eased himself down to the soft mattress. When finally he was lying on his side, he lay still, breathing heavily. Beads of sweat coated his forehead and neck.

Anna gently combed through his hair with her fingers. "Think you'll be okay now?"

He closed his eyes and slowly nodded.

Anna quietly left the room and went to the kitchen where Liesel was preparing a late dinner for themselves. Frank was sitting on a chair and talking to her.

"We've decided we better take turns checking Colsson during the night," Liesel told her. "Someone should check him every two hours. I'll check him at ten o'clock."

"I'll check him at twelve."

"Your father can check at two, then I'll go at four."

"Okay. That leaves me checking at six." Anna sighed and prayed silently. *Please be with him tonight.*

Walt came over two days after Colsson got home. Anna was changing Colsson's bandages when Frank led him in. Colsson was still very weak, and his exhaustion and minimal motion showed it if he was up for too long.

"Hi, Colsson," Walt greeted. "How are you doing?"

Colsson smiled up at his brother. "I'm doing alright, Walt."

Anna finished fastening the end of the bandage. "There. You're done." She smiled at Colsson.

The bandages swathed Colsson's body beginning under his arms and went down to his waist.

Walt sat on the bed next to Colsson. "You're looking a lot better than you were at the hospital."

"I know," Colsson replied. "I'm better because I'm here and not at the hospital. I was having a hard time there. I was pretty scared."

Walt squeezed Colsson's shoulder gently. "I know you were. But you're here now."

Colsson chuckled weakly.

"No nurses coming in all the time and poking at ya," Walt added teasingly.

"Well, one still does, but somehow I don't mind this one so much." He fixated his gaze on Anna, who was standing by a tall nightstand a short distance from the bed and writing in a notebook; recording the time she had changed the bandages and how the scars had looked.

She felt Colsson looking at her and turned her head. "What?"

"I was telling Walt I didn't mind a certain nurse coming in all the time and poking at me."

"And you meant me?" Anna asked with a slight chuckle.

"Who else would you think?" Colsson asked with a smile.

"Hey, I'm not a nurse," Anna laughed. She came to stand next to Colsson.

Colsson squeezed her hand and looked up at her, a smile on his face. "You're the perfect one."

Anna ruffled Colsson's hair. "I'll talk to you boys later," she said as she left the room.

Walt asked, "Do you think Frank will hire me?"

"As a ranch hand?" asked Colsson in surprise.

"Yep. That way I can be near you. I need to get a job anyway."

"Maybe," Colsson said thoughtfully. "You could try. It would be wonderful to have my brother here."

"I'm going to. I'll talk to Frank about it after lunch."

"Sounds good to me," Colsson replied. Then he grew sober. "Walt, tell me, is there any way someone like me can be with a girl for the rest of his life?"

"Sure," Walt replied. "Through marriage."

Colsson fiddled with his fingers. "Marriage." He sighed. "I was afraid of that."

"Why do you say that?"

"I just don't know if I can. My background is so messed up. I feel like I am not capable of marrying anyone."

"I wouldn't say that."

"It's a big responsibility," Colsson said quietly. "Is it worth it if you really love that woman?"

"Yes," Walt replied. "There will be hard times in your family, as there is in everyone's life. There will be nothing you can do to escape the hard times. But the joy and love will outweigh it all. The Christian trusts God and looks to Him for help through all times, good or bad."

Colsson nodded. "I want to marry her, but how can I go about it?"

"Whoa, hold on," Walt chuckled. "The first thing you have to do, before you do *anything*, you have to talk to Anna's father."

"What do I talk to him about?"

"Perhaps you should first tell him how you feel about Anna. I believe he will guide you in the right direction."

Colsson nodded again. "Anything for Anna. I'll tell Frank immediately."

Walt put his hand on Colsson's shoulder. "That's a good idea. But not when Anna's around. Wait to talk to Frank when you're alone with him."

"You'll help me, won't you?" Colsson pleaded.

Walt shook his head. "I'm afraid I can't, Colsson. This is something you have to do on your own."

Liesel poked her head in the room. "Hey, you two, lunch is ready."

Walt stood and offered his hand to Colsson. Colsson took it, and carefully stood. Walt helped Colsson get a shirt on, then the Helder brothers went to the dining room. Some of the guests plied Colsson with questions about where had he been, why was he here and his family wasn't, why he didn't often eat, and who was this person with him. He didn't want to answer all the questions. The confusion in his mind grew with each second.

"I'd...I'd rather not talk about it," he confessed in a murmur. "Please don't ask me."

The questions immediately stopped. They regarded Colsson and each other with curious looks before returning to normal conversations.

Colsson gave a small sigh as he nervously clutched and wrung his hands on his lap.

Walt leaned closer to Colsson. "Something wrong?"

Colsson nodded. "I hate all the questions."

"Makes sense. I don't blame you, but I don't blame them. They wouldn't ask if they didn't care about you."

After lunch, Walt and Colsson went out to the barnyard where Frank and the two ranch hands were standing and talking. Jack had grown quieter since breaking off with Anna.

"Hi, Walt and Colsson," Frank said as they walked up.

"Are you in need of an extra man, Frank?" asked Walt.

"I don't think so, why?"

"I wanted to see if I could work for you if you did," Walt replied, his heart sinking.

Frank turned to Jack and Jake. "What do you fellows think? How are you two handling things?"

Jake looked at Jack. "We typically can handle most things by ourselves, but we can have a tough time keeping up with fencing, herding horses, and such."

"Need an extra ranch hand?"

"We were actually going to discuss it with you, sir," said Jack. "We might need some extra help, for sure."

"Hired," said Frank, turning back to Walt. "And as soon as you're well enough, Colsson, I'll hire you, too."

"Thank you," said Walt joyfully.

"Jack and Jake, would you show Walt where the bunkhouse is and teach him the routine?"

"Sure thing," said Jake.

Jack and Jake led Walt toward the bunkhouse.

Colsson stayed quiet. His heart pounded within his chest. Here was his chance to talk to Frank about Anna. After Jack, Jake, and Walt disappeared, Frank asked, "Glad to see you up and out here."

"I hate being in my room all the time. Too many bad memories. So I'm trying to get out more," said Colsson.

"Something on your mind?"

How did you know? Colsson wondered silently. He swallowed and threw a glance back at the house. "Anna," he whispered.

"What about her?" Frank gently prompted.

"I want to marry her," Colsson said quietly.

Frank's heart jumped. "You can't just marry someone, Colsson. You have a lot to learn before I will even consider letting you court her."

"I will learn," said Colsson, "for her sake."

Frank put his hand on Colsson's shoulder. "Let's get back in. Anna will be wondering where you are. You don't want to worry her about you."

"That's the last thing I want," Colsson said anxiously. He quickened his pace toward the house.

"Slow down, Colsson," Frank chuckled. "You're *definitely* going to worry her if you come in bleeding."

Reluctantly, Colsson slowed down and walked with Frank back to the house.

Chapter Fourteen

"No, no, no!" Esau screamed. "No! Please, no! Lord, I believe!"

A door closed in Esau's face.

"I NEVER KNEW YOU," The Lord said sadly from behind the door.

Esau banged on the door that stood between him and eternal life. "I believe!" he shouted again.

"I GAVE YOU MULTIPLE CHANCES IN YOUR LIFE, ESAU," God replied. "BUT YOU CHOSE TO IGNORE ME. I GAVE MY SON TO BE PUNISHED FOR YOUR SINS NOT LONG AGO. I TRIED EVERYTHING IN YOUR LIFE TO BRING YOU TO ME," He sighed. "I WANTED NOTHING MORE THAN TO HOLD YOU IN MY ARMS AT THIS MOMENT AND CALL YOU MY CHILD. I WANTED TO TELL YOU HOW MUCH I LOVE YOU. I WANTED *YOU*. BUT YOU DID NOT LISTEN TO ME. YOU GAVE IN TO HATE, SATAN'S SIDE." God's voice shook off the sorrow and turned angry.

"MY HOLY HOME WILL NOT BE DIRTIED BY THE BLOOD OF A WILLING AND UNREPENTANT SINNER. YOU WILL BE PAID IN FULL FOR YOUR WICKEDNESS. DEPART FROM ME."

Esau flung himself at the door again. An angel tackled him from behind. Desperately, Esau tried to wrench free from his adversary, but he was no match for the angel. A shrill scream made Esau pause and listen. What was happening? The angel took advantage of the split-second distraction. Quickly he gripped Esau by the shoulders and marched him forward.

An unbearable, sulfurous stench greeted Esau and a blast of heat struck him full in the face. He put up his arm to block the heat, but it did little good to ward off the heat. His captor marched him on nonetheless.

To where? Esau wondered.

Another blast of heat nearly stifled Esau. Up ahead was a huge lake, but there was something strange about it. Instead of the blue friendliness of an ordinary lake, this one was filled with hot, furious, bubbling lava. He could hear cursing and swearing that he had never heard before. Desperate gasps for air reached his ears. A black figure popped up near the edge of hell. Esau almost screamed when the figure turned his head to look in his direction. The face of the figure was charred black, the eyes rolled in his head, and the hair had completely burned from the figure's scalp. Skin fell away from the figure's face and neck. The head sagged and lolled from side to side. The figure released a bloodcurdling cry, his jaw dropping to extreme depth as he grasped for the side of the lake. An angel came running around the lake and unsheathed his sword. One slice went right through the figure's arms. The tortured creature let out a long, pain filled scream and slid back under the burning waves. The bloody arms, now gone from the person, lay on the ground where the person had been trying to climb out from hell. The angel kicked them back into the sulfurous lake. A burst of flame engulfed the helpless person, devouring and drowning him down beneath the depths of hell's fury.

Out of the corner of his eye, Esau caught a glimpse of his dad flying through the air and landing in the lake! He gasped and turned his head. He saw another angel pushing his brother towards the lake! Yet another angel ran to Saul. Together, the two angels lifted the fighting and screaming Saul and heaved him into the lake. Saul fell headfirst, still screaming, into the lake.

"Saul!" Esau shrieked. He tried to run towards his brother, but the angel holding onto him gripped him even tighter. The angel who assisted in throwing Saul ran over to where Esau was.

All at once, Esau understood. He fought fiercely with the angel, but it was too late. He felt himself lifting off the ground and hurling through the air. The scorching, blazing fire choked off the scream that had risen to his throat. Down deep beneath the surface of the furious fire Esau sank. His feet touched the bottom. He pushed off and clawed for the surface. He felt an extremely hot, burning sensation all over, and it kept getting worse by the second. Esau didn't know how much longer he could hold out in the blazing heat.

At last, he broke the surface. He gasped for air, but he couldn't breathe right. His lungs felt compressed, crushing all the air and the ability to breathe from them. His entire body felt as though it were on fire.

Trying to stay afloat with his legs and one arm, he clawed at his face with his other hand, trying to relieve the heat that intensely stuck to his face. A fingernail snagged a rip in his forehead. Pain shot through his whole head and, with a loud, terrible, ripping sound, the flesh from the left half of his face fell into his hand. Esau gasped in horror as he looked at the large flap of skin in his hand. He could see the outline of his eye, nose, mouth, and chin on it. The skin was burned completely black. The flesh dripped blood down into his hand and from his hand into the fire! Suddenly, the flesh erupted in flame and was consumed before his very eyes! He touched his face. Pain tingled through his head as he felt his skull. His eye on the side that the flesh had come off was missing. He stuck his finger into his eyeball socket. He heard a sandpaper-scratching-like sound as he rubbed ashes and blood from the bony curves of the socket.

He screamed relentlessly, not believing that this was happening. He glanced at his left arm. Only then did he realize that his arm was charred, and charred flesh fell into the fire in front of him. Flame licked his fingers and crept up his arm until his entire arm was devoured.

Esau sank beneath the churning waves once more. Again, his feet touched the bottom, but this time his knees buckled forcefully, and intense pain that he had never felt before shot through his whole body as his knees hit the bottom. Every limb felt weak and was in such severe pain that Esau finally gave up fighting to reach the surface. There was no way even the toughest person on earth could survive this.

As he floated to the top, Esau drew in breath and gazed at his legs. He gasped. His lower legs were no longer there! His legs from the knee down had fallen off when his knees buckled. Searing, fierce pain shot through him again. He looked just in time to see his thighs fall away from his hips! Through the blood and flesh of his thighs, which were now floating away from him, he could see the ball joint from where it had detached. He grit his teeth and glanced to his right and to his left. He stared at himself in pure, abject horror. Not only were his legs now gone, but *both* of his arms were missing! The rest of his body was on fire!

Adding to Esau's pain and misery was the realization that he had fallen prey to Satan, the devil, and had willingly abandoned God the Father. He was being paid back for his evilness and stupidity during his life. He cried aloud with all the breath in his lungs. He wanted nothing more than to return to the arms of Jesus Christ. Instead, he knew he must stay here for forever.

Esau's agony was far beyond what the world had ever known. He sank below the crashing waves of fire, overcome by the powers of the second death. *Hell!*

Thud! Esau opened his eyes. He looked all around. The familiar walls of the prison surrounded him. No waves of fire engulfed him, no one was screaming, yelling, or even crying. In fact, everything was still and quiet. He wiggled his shoulders. A tingling feeling swept down his arms and landed in his fingertips. He moved his hips and knees. The same thing happened for his legs. He reached cautiously and hesitantly to touch his face. He expected to feel his bloody skull from where the flesh tore away from the bone. Instead, his face was intact, and he had both eyes. He didn't have so much as a scratch anywhere.

Esau lay still and tried to piece things together in his mind. He remembered everything perfectly. He came to the realization that he had just had a nightmare, but the whole thing seemed too real and life-like to be just a nightmare.

Esau began shaking uncontrollably in fear. He forced himself to be still.

"God," he whispered softly and with all his heart. "I ask for forgiveness for my cruel ways. I don't know I why I thought it was okay to treat Colsson so badly but I'm sorry I did. God, please forgive me, and bring me back to You. I have forgotten You, but I am here. Take me back."

Tears ran down Esau's face as he pleaded and begged God's forgiveness. Terrible heartache over his past wrongdoings filled him to the top. Doubt that he could ever be forgiven made him feel worse.

"REMEMBER PAUL. WHAT YOU HAVE DONE IS NOTHING NEXT TO WHAT SAUL OF TARSUS HAD DONE. BUT I SAVED HIM, BECAUSE IT WAS IN MY HEART TO DO SO. I HAD GREATER PLANS IN MIND. I HAVE DONE THIS BEFORE, AND I WILL DO IT AGAIN."

Peace flooded through Esau, chasing away all doubt from his mind. "God, forgive me, and help me live as You would have me live."

"YOU ARE FORGIVEN."

Those little words, though spoken so softly, had such a powerful effect on Esau. The remaining fear from his nightmare left him, and his eyes closed in a deep sleep as his heart lifted.

Saul awoke from the same nightmare of hell. "God, what was it?" he asked, shaking.

"THAT, IS WHERE YOU WILL SPEND ETERNITY."

"Oh, no, oh no, no, no!" Saul whispered to himself, for once somber. Fear and dread took hold. "God, please have mercy on my soul!"

"I AM WILLING TO BRING YOU BACK TO ME, IF YOU WILL ONLY REPENT."

To Saul, the word sounded eerie, and ominous. "Repent?"

"REMEMBER YOUR WRONGDOINGS, REGRET THEM WITH ALL YOUR HEART, AND VOW NEVER TO GO BACK. IF YOU WILL COME BACK TO ME, I WILL SAVE YOU. I WILL FORGIVE YOU, AND CALL YOU MINE."

Saul thought over everything wrong he had done in his life. He shook his head. "God, there's no way the kindest person could overlook all I have done."

"AH, BUT I WILL. LOVE HAS CONQUERED, AND IT IS THE ONE THING I GIVE FREELY TO ALL, REGARDLESS OF REPENTANCE, OR STUBBORN REFUSAL AND IGNORANCE. THERE IS NO THING, NO SIN, NO BURDEN, NO AMOUNT OF REJECTION THAT TAKES YOU WHERE I CANNOT FIND YOU. COME BACK, AND I WILL RELEASE YOU, AND FORGIVE YOU."

"Here I am, God. Make me clean again."

"MERCY AND GRACE ARE YOURS, NOW. YOU ARE FORGIVEN."

Saul slipped into a quiet and joyous sleep, grateful to be forgiven, even though he felt he didn't deserve it. Love was a wondrous thing.

Timothy's eyes flew open and he gave a startled gasp. Sweat poured down his face and neck. Violent shakes seized him. "G-G-G-God! P-p-p-please have m-m-mercy! Sp-sp-spare me!"

"CRUEL MAN. WHY SHOULD I SPARE YOU?"

Timothy shook even worse, and he felt himself sinking into despair. Fear tore into him. Regret, desperation, and failing hopes fell into his tormented mind. Visions of the nightmare flashed before him.

"God, please! I never would have gone down this path had I known what lays at the end. I would have been careful to follow You!"

"MEND YOUR EVIL WAYS, AND RETURN TO ME. THAT IS ALL I ASK OF YOU. THAT IS ALL I ASK OF ANYONE, AND EVERYONE. MERCY AND GRACE I HOLD IN MY HAND."

"But how can you gift to me mercy and grace after all I have done?"

"THEY ARE MINE TO GIVE TO WHOM I WILL. I WILL GLADLY GIVE TO THOSE WHO ASK, AND WHO ASK WITH ALL THEIR HEARTS. THEY ARE YOURS NOW."

"But how can that be?"

"BECAUSE OF LOVE."

"God, I cannot bear the thought of remaining in such a place for eternity. I humbly ask, though I do not deserve it, please take me back."

"YOU ARE FORGIVEN, MY SON."

Peace dominated over Timothy's once cruel heart. Grateful tears slid down his cheeks. He thought over what would have happened if he hadn't had the dream. He might have continued in evil for the rest of his life.

"God didn't want that to happen," he murmured. "Not to me. I wish everyone who leads the kind of life I did received that dream. I wish they could come the Father as I have when they are given the chance."

"KNOW ALSO, TIMOTHY, YOU WILL SEE KELLY AGAIN."

Kelly's image filled Timothy's mind. Through his closed eyes, he saw Kelly moving, laughing, playing. "Kelly," he murmured. A smile crossed his lips. "Kelly." Joy at the thought of seeing Kelly again erupted in his heart, and he no longer answered to hate's call.

Chapter Fifteen

Sunlight streamed in the window and played its gentle rays on Anna's face, waking her up. More than a year had passed by since Colsson's abuse had ended.

Today was a snowy October day. It was October 21, Anna's birthday. She lay in the bed and thought for a little while about the events of the past year and the months she had been courting Colsson.

Colsson was able to work harder now that his back was doing quite a bit better with healing. Although his back was forever horribly scarred, it no longer bothered him much. Occasionally he'd work too hard, and the scars would break open. Still, Frank taught him to drive and do many other things.

She smiled as she thought about how much he'd changed, then leaped from her bed. The wood floor was cold on her bare feet. She always liked that feeling of the boards in the wintertime. Quickly she dressed and went to the kitchen.

Colsson was already in the kitchen along with Frank and Liesel. Even though he was now one of the ranch hands, he slept inside so that Anna and Liesel could take care of his back when there was a need for it. Normally, he ate out in the bunkhouse with the other ranch hands, but on this special morning, he came in for Anna's birthday.

The trio looked up and smiled as Anna entered the kitchen. "Happy Birthday, Anna!" they said together.

Anna took her place at the table. "Thank you," she said happily.

They spent a long time together talking after breakfast was over. At last when Liesel got up to clear the table off, Colsson leaned in close and asked, "Anna, would you like to go for a moonlight ride tonight?"

"I would love to!"

"After dinner, then?"

"Sure!"

The day passed in a busy blur although there were no more boarders at the ranch. Horse needed to be taken care of and the ones in the barn exercised. While the horses were given a run, the barn was cleaned out, and hay put down in the stalls for bedding.

"Anna, you haven't forgotten our ride tonight, have you?" Colsson asked teasingly that night after Anna had opened her gifts.

Anna teased back. "Oh, dear. I'm afraid I did forget. Is it too late?"

He nodded slowly. "Yes, it is. We'll have to put it off until the next full moon."

She tried to frown at him, but he burst into laughter. It was impossible for Anna to hold the face that she was making, and she burst into laughter. They slouched on the couch and laughed even harder whenever he slowed down long enough to see her face.

Colsson felt wonderful inside. He had never had a reason to laugh as hard as he was now.

"You two better get dressed if you're going to go on that ride tonight," Liesel said, giggling. Even Frank was chuckling.

"Are you ready, Anna?" Colsson asked.

Anna looked down at herself. "Do I look ready to you?"

He tried hard to keep himself from laughing. "Not really," he replied.

Anna chuckled. She rushed off to get her winter gear for riding.

A few minutes later, they were saddling their horses in the corral. Snowflakes became visible as they emerged from the sea of black clouds overhead. Anna held onto Emerald's bridle and looked up at the sky. She loved riding in the winter when it was snowing. She mounted her horse and waited for Colsson. He checked something in his pocket and then mounted Butterscotch. They trotted their horses to Anna's treehouse. They dismounted and stood in front of their horses. Anna took off her hat to let the snow fall onto her black hair.

He held her close to his chest for a long time until slowly the snow ceased and the moon appeared.

"I love you, Anna," he whispered. "You brought life back into me when I was dead in heart." From his pocket, he took a tiny package which he gave to her.

Hesitantly, Anna took it, removed her gloves, and tore the wrapping with her fingernail. Inside was a tiny box.

Colsson held his breath as his gaze went back and forth from Anna's face and back down at the box.

Anna's fingers shook as she pried the hinged lid open. In the moonlight, the shape of a simple, but pretty silver ring stood out plainly.

"Col-" Anna choked. Her hand trembled.

Colsson took the little box from Anna and removed the ring from the box. He tenderly slid the beautiful ring onto her finger.

She looked up at him, too stunned to speak. Bright moonlight glinted off the snow that had fallen on Colsson's blond hair.

"Anna," he whispered. The words wouldn't form in his throat, but Anna understood.

"Yes," she whispered back.

Ever so tenderly, Colsson touched her cold cheek and kissed her. Swept away in the moment, the kiss made her forget everything from the outside world. All that mattered to her was right in front of her.

The rapture of holding a woman in his arms was a joy Colsson had never known in his life. Every trouble from his past that had ever threatened to haunt him faded. He knew what love really meant.

He forced himself to pull away a couple inches. "I never want to leave, but I told your father and mother we would be back within two hours."

"I don't want to leave either. Can't we stay here and look at the moon for a little while?"

"Yes, of course we can." He put his arm around her shoulders and together, they gazed up at the moon. Clouds passed over it, dimming its glow. The soft, silent snow fell on and around them, glistening in the remaining moonlight. She breathed and watched the steam float away until it disappeared. This was the most beautiful night they'd ever seen. Neither of them wanted this moment to pass away.

Several minutes came and went before they laughingly decided to leave. The ride back to the ranch house was lively. They discussed and joked about wedding plans. They considered pranks to pull such as putting plain grape juice in wine bottles.

Anna was too excited and happy to sleep. She stared out the window at the moon and the blanket of white. She constantly gazed down at her hand to assure herself the beautiful ring still clung to her finger. A moonbeam glinted off the silver ring. The ring would always remain there, no matter what.

Colsson also ignored sleep's call. He lay in his bed, staring up at the ceiling. Who knew someone as rejected as himself would be loved as he was, and have someone to love? The ways of the Lord were blessed indeed. A verse from Psalms popped into his mind.

Psalm 10: 17-18, *'Lord, Thou hast heard the desire of the poor; Thou prepares their heart; Thou bendest Thine ear to them,*

To judge the fatherless and poor, that earthly man cause them to fear no more.'

"How true," Colsson whispered to himself. "Even through ten years of waiting, God was still listening and making ready to help me in His own good time. Just as Anna told me, though I was not willing to believe it for a long time."

Colsson clutched Anna's hand tightly and the two of them ducked their heads to avoid the flower petals flying as they made their way to their vehicle. Anna hiked her wedding gown skirts higher and shrieked with delight as Colsson pulled her along. The wedding day had come at last.

Liesel held a tissue to her nose as the couple drove away. A lump settled in Frank's throat. What had happened to their daughter who, just a few years ago it seemed, claimed she would never marry; she would stay at the ranch all her life?

Jack stood and watched Anna and Colsson leaving, his heart at last free from the burden of parting with Anna. Beside him stood Terra. The young woman put a hand on his shoulder. Sun glinted off the diamond ring on her finger, placed there during a dance only a short while earlier. "So when is ours going to be?" she asked with a smile.

Jack turned to smile at her. "Within the next few months, I hope, darling." He squeezed her hand and tucked her arm under his.

They watched Anna and Colsson wave goodbye to the crowd until their vehicle faded from sight.

The next morning, Anna and Colsson awoke early. Quickly they packed their things together, ate breakfast, and left the hotel.

During their long, all-day drive through the spring colors and the signs of new life, the newlyweds discussed their own new life. For countless hours, they talked and planned of a home and children.

As evening approached, Colsson stopped at a beautiful campsite near a quiet river. Wildlife played in the bushes and trees. A gentle breeze blew across the water and moved through the grass, rustling it. Colsson put his arm around his wife and together they walked along the river. They stopped at the top of a small hill near their campsite. From the hilltop, they had a bright and clear view of the evening sunset.

The whole broad sky was streaked in orange, purple, pink, and red. A true sight wondrous to behold, especially with love written above it, below it, and in it. For who could have the love to design it other than the same one Who had love to give to the earth love, free for all those who look, and ask. Only One could have the love to lay out the sunset and order every detail of it. Only One could have the love to take away the greatest burden humans could ever know. Only One can love all people, even those like Colsson, no matter what they have done.

"Oh Colsson, what a glorious sunset!" Anna exclaimed.

"It is beautiful," Colsson agreed. "but not as beautiful as you are."

She smiled sweetly and crossed her hands in front of her. He put his arm around her and laid his hand on her shoulder. Together they watched the sun slowly sink and display bright, beautiful colors across the sky.

"This past year, I have been turned from a miserable wretch into a God-fearing man. If God hadn't brought you into my life, Anna, I would have died long ago. Who would have thought that an utterly filthy and faithless boy would have such wonderful things happen to him?"

"I feel the same way. You've changed a lot in the months that we've been together."

"I am a witness of love. Not only am I now loved by a woman, but I have witnessed the love of Jesus Christ. I just can't believe the incredible love I have experienced. I was so rejected, so alone, and so miserable that I never thought that anyone, even God, could ever love me." He paused and turned her to face him. "You proved to me that I was wrong in my way of thinking. I'll forever be grateful to you for that. I love you, Anna, and I'll always love you."

Her heart was so full she felt a tear slip free. "I love you, Colsson. And I'll always love you."

He put both of his arms around her, and she put her hands on his shoulders. With all the love they had to offer each other, Anna and Colsson kissed. As they stood in the gorgeous evening, God's voice spoke to them from the direction of the setting sun.

"WELL DONE, MY CHILDREN. MY BLESSINGS TO YOU, AND REMEMBER THAT I WILL ALWAYS LOVE YOU FOREVER."

The End

CPSIA information can be obtained
at www.ICGtesting.com
Printed in the USA
BVHW030028050422
633291BV00021B/262

9 781736 384220